STORM CLOUD

J.S. JASPER

Copyright © [2023] by [J.S. Jasper]

All rights reserved.

The characters and events portrayed in this book are fictitious. Any similarity to real persons, living or dead, is coincidental and not intended by the author.

No part of this book may be reproduced, or stored in a retrieval system, or transmitted in any form or by any means, electronic, mechanical, photocopying, recording, or otherwise, without express written permission of the publisher.

Cover Designer: Roy Nottage

Editor: R. A. Wright Editing

Formatter: KB. Row

PORLOCK
01/24

Please return/renew this item by the last date shown on this label, or on your self-service receipt.

To renew this item, visit **www.librarieswest.org.uk** or contact your library

Your borrower number and PIN are required.

It's always a love story.

Chapter One

There's nothing Sophie enjoys more than a bright, sunny winter morning, where the last of the red leaves scatter the pavement. She loves the way she can see her own breath as she bunches her shoulders to hide her face in her knitted red scarf. She loves the way people's cheeks turn pink from the cold, and the smell of peppermint hot chocolate in the air. She loves when she can sit in her bookstore with a to-do list she's allowed to ignore and a mug of tea in her hand. Winter is her favorite time of year.

Shame those days are few and far between.

It's a gray, cold winter afternoon when Sophie smiles for the first time that day. It might be because she finally had the radiators replaced in her bookstore, so it's no longer freezing the second it hits October. She can sit behind her counter with a book, only in a thick jumper (even though it's starting to snow outside), and ignore the growing list of errands she needs to complete.

It might be because she took the first sip of a new flavor of tea and decided it already ranks third on her list of top teas.

It might even be because her order of new books came in this morning, and one of her favorite things to do is look at the pretty covers before they're sold and her customers add their own message inside before giving it to that special person in their life.

It's probably because she saw a man slip on the icy sidewalk and he looked a little like a cartoon character. He's fine, obviously—he didn't even hit the floor. It barely holds her attention for longer than four seconds. Instead, her eyes drift to the dusting of snow collecting on the outside of the wooden window frames. If the snow lasts long enough, she might even remove the fake snow she used to decorate the store windows two months ago in preparation for Christmas.

Still, Sophie lets her smile linger, holding on to the warm feeling until she feels she's probably acting a bit creepy. She's not sure how else to get through Christmas and New Year's to February if not for romanticizing the little things. The red noses of people rushing to buy a book for a loved one, or the teenage girl who comes in every Saturday with exactly the right change for the next installment in the fantasy series Sophie read when she was a child.

She tries to find something good in everyone that comes into the shop, though she'll never tell them any of these things. They're a secret, just for her. And if that fails, she'll stretch her imagination to the people walking past.

Her secret weapon to get through life is to find the happy little things and keep them close to her chest so she never has to share her happiness with anyone. Because if she shares them, they can take them from her. Besides, then she might actually have to talk to someone, and she's not about to do that if she can help it.

Sometimes it's harder than she would like. Like when there's a parent who doesn't really interact with their child when they're clearly so excited about what they want to read. At least they're reading at all! When that happens, Sophie slips a cute bookmark between the pages of their book and imagines how their face will light up when they find it later.

Sometimes, though, sometimes it's way too easy to find things to like. For example, the guy that just barreled through the door, almost sending the bell flying. He has a smattering of freckles on the bridge of his nose, and freckles are one of Sophie's favorite things. And that isn't even the best thing about him!

His chestnut hair is wild like he just took off a hat, even though she can't see one in his hands. His nose is red, and he keeps scrunching it in a way that suggests he's trying to warm it up. He stumbles over his own feet as he shakes the snow from his broad shoulders. The shop brightens with every step he takes.

He's adorable.

Sophie wonders what he's here for. His eyes fly across the shelves so fast he can't possibly be reading any of the titles, but she doesn't mind. She watches his eyes widen with every step he takes to get closer to her register. The store isn't huge—two main aisles stacked high with new and second-hand books—so it doesn't take him long to get to her.

His eyes widen further as he stops in front of her, like he was expecting the shop to be unmanned or something. Maybe he wasn't ready to talk to anyone.

"Hi, hello . . . erm," he stutters, gripping his backpack like he also has no idea why he's here.

"Hi," Sophie replies, placing her bookmark back and giving him her best customer service face. (It's a look of being aggressively bored, obviously.) "Can I help you?"

The question seems to shake him out of his thoughts, and he shakes his head as well. It's frustratingly cute—an emotion Sophie tries not to place on the random customer she's never going to see again.

"I really need the Advanced Chemistry textbook, please, because I'm going to fail my class for sure . . . for sure, for sure," he says, his hands fidgeting nervously. His brows furrow further with every word.

As Sophie watches him, she tries to work out if he is actually college-age. Though he has a slight baby face, there's no way he's under twenty. Then again, he might be, and that would mean he's *way* too young for her. Not that it matters—she wouldn't talk to him outside of the store anyway. He seems oblivious to her inner turmoil as he continues.

"But the library doesn't have any copies left, and my exam is in like two weeks, and I'm so screwed. Marriot is definitely going to drop me from his class . . . " His eyes are still wide and his cheeks pink, and Sophie would, for reasons unconfirmed, give him everything the store sold if it helped him. "So, I was hoping you sold it?" he asks, rubbing his lips together.

Sophie desperately wants to help him. Because she's a great bookstore owner, or because her heart has been pitter-pattering far too hard in her chest since he walked through the door?

"You know they're like two hundred dollars, right?"

He winces like he did know that, and she feels a little bad for him, though the library always runs out of that book. She knows because she took the same course five years ago, so she also knows if he'd been at the library anytime this term, he probably would have figured that out and got there early enough to get it.

"I know . . . I just *have* to pass this class. I'm already years behind everyone else, and if I fail . . . " He shakes his head again and pulls his wallet out of his back pocket. Years behind everyone else . . . so maybe not as young as she first thought.

It doesn't matter. She doesn't sell it anyway.

Sophie grimaces. "I don't sell textbooks. Sorry."

She neglects to mention that she might have the textbook he's after under her counter right now, because she keeps all her old textbooks in the store in case she needs to prop up a shelf. But she's also not entirely bothered whether or not he fails . . .

Probably . . .

If she lies to herself . . .

"Oh, man," he grumbles, pushing his hand through his hair. "That's alright. Um, I can just wing it, right?"

"You want to just 'wing' a project that's worth forty percent of your grade?" she asks, her brow arched. It's unkind. He just said he didn't have the book, and she's not planning on giving it to him, even if she does have it under her desk. Besides, he's only trying to make himself feel better.

"Um, aren't you supposed to agree with me?" he asks, frowning at her, but the playfulness in his tone is reflected in his face. She's not sure he could be serious if he tried, and she's only known him for three minutes. The smile he'd been hiding since he started his fake-complaining takes over, and he gives her a stunning grin. The motion makes her throat go dry, the corded muscles of his neck begging her to trace her fingers down his throat. She shrugs instead, her fingers gripping the edges of her book a little too hard so her eyes don't linger on his dimple.

"I am burdened with telling the truth."

He smiles at her again, a softer one this time, and his eyes crinkle at the edges despite what she said not being all that funny and definitely true.

She decides he looks like sunshine. The kind she had wanted to see this morning when her alarm went off. The kind that would have made her day just a tad better. The kind she didn't know she missed until he walked into the store. But his slightly pink cheeks and disheveled hair won't make her a liar. So, she stands her ground until he speaks again.

"But the customer is always right," he replies, his thick brows furrowing in mock annoyance. He's not a particularly good actor; his jaw twitches with his obvious need to smile. She enjoys how clearly he's trying to mess with her, like he's not entirely sure he's allowed to talk to her (even if he is doing so with a nervous energy she'd be blind to miss).

"You haven't even bought anything. You're the worst customer I've had today," Sophie says back, her finger flipping the page of her book over as if she's read a single word since he walked in.

"Hmm," he grumbles, his lips pouting. He looks around, his eyes sparkling when he spots her collection of bookmarks. She won't tell him she designs them, because she hasn't told anyone that, not even her mom, and she's the only person on earth who really knows her.

Instead, she pulls her lower lip between her teeth to stop smiling when his fingers dust over the ribbons while he chooses between designs.

"One, please," he says, pulling one out and placing it on the counter.

"Good choice," she says, looking at the wildflower placeholder. Her finger runs along the light smattering of forget-me-nots, the different pink hues making her as happy as they did when she first put pen to paper.

"Yeah?" he asks, as if her approval of his design choice is the best thing that's happened to him today.

"Yeah."

She wraps it in tissue paper—white, of course—and rings him up. He's still smiling at her, and she's not sure what to do about it because it makes her heart thump whenever she looks up at him, and he's already looking at her.

"Three ninety-nine, please."

He hands her a five, and she takes the time to dutifully count his change as she wills herself to calm down—he's just a cute guy she's never going to see again. Her fingers brush his palm when she passes his money back, and she hopes the dim store lights and the gray skies mean he can't see her blushing. He immediately shoves it into her—thankfully empty—tea mug.

"You know that's not a tip jar, right?" she asks, her head cocked to the side as he flounders.

"Oh, well, I tipped anyway, so . . . "

"So?"

"I'm your favorite customer of the day, right?" he asks, his brows high, like he's not sure if she'll say yes or no.

"Hmm," she replies, crossing her arms over her chest. The way he effortlessly brings her playful side out isn't lost on her, nor is the loud laugh he lets out at her pouting.

"You have to tell me I won't fail now!"

"I don't have to do anything," she replies. Her tone is the same as it always is when she's talking to strangers, customers, or anyone that's not her mom, if she's honest, but she internally recoils all the same. It's around now (no more than ten minutes, usually) that someone decides they don't like her. That maybe she's rude, even though she doesn't mean to be—she was just being truthful.

Not that she would expect anyone to have formed an actual opinion of a stranger in under ten minutes—as if she hasn't got many thoughts about the guy in front of her, but that's neither here nor there—but someone can decide if she's worth their time or not in hardly any time at all. Sometimes, it's clear people aren't attracted to her personality, which is rude, because she's hilarious, but they will power through her sarcasm and eye rolls because they find her attractive.

Sophie doesn't care either way, but she would prefer to know if someone is being nice to her because they want to be—not because they think they might get something out of it. Either way, she regrets the way she spoke, even if she shouldn't.

He doesn't seem to mind, though. His smile never falters.

"You're right," he agrees, with a shrug. He leans in slightly, the smell of his aftershave invading her senses. She'll probably dream about it later. "What if I buy two?"

He ponders the bookmarks for a little longer, and she appreciates the effort he takes to look like he's not about to throw them in the bottom of his bag the second he leaves.

"Which one is your favorite?" he asks, his brown eyes flicking up to hold her gaze for a beat too long, then back to the task at hand.

Sophie doesn't like to tell people things. She values keeping information to herself in case anyone finds something to use against her. There's probably a reason she's terrified to give someone any piece of her in case they decide they actually don't want it, but she's not going to try to figure that out in her bookstore at one p.m. on a Thursday.

So, she doesn't let the information slip. Not even her favorite bookmark. It's her entire personality, really. That and romance books. And early noughties R & B. And lasagna. And a good mascara.

"I like all of them," she replies. It's not a lie, of course, and, though he won't know it, it's the most personal thing she's told anyone in years.

"My favorite is this one," he replies, twisting the bookmark he just purchased from her in his fingers. It's her favorite too. "But this one is pretty as well," he says, picking up the blue one with yellow daffodils. It is pretty, she thinks. She did design them, after all, so she's biased in thinking they're all nice for different reasons. It's nice to hear it from someone else. He continues before she says anything, which she's grateful for, because sometimes speaking is just too hard.

"I mean, they're all pretty, obviously!" he stammers, his eyes wide as he blushes slightly. It makes her smile. It doesn't require a spoken response, not really. His face settles as she smiles at him, so she could leave it there, but something in her wants to give him just a little more than she gives anyone else. It's silly.

But she does it anyway.

"Obviously," she says. And he smiles.

Chapter Two

The monthly orders are finally in, and Sophie almost does a tiny dance in the middle of the store. It's been a busy few months. The Christmas period near kills her every year (she's only had the store two years, but two for two—she can't argue with the stats) and then people have New Year's resolutions to read more books or lose weight or cook more, which mainly means people buy more books. By the time February rolls around, she's wiped out and wants to say "what a year" every three seconds when it's barely a third of the way over.

But she's feeling better today than she has done in the past weeks. She could say it's the order arriving, or the new jam she tried on her toast this morning (cherry), or the lingering thoughts of the guy with slightly curly hair yesterday (even if she did check whether her textbook was the right one as soon as he left yesterday, and it wasn't). It doesn't really matter what it is. She's in a great mood.

So, she does the only thing she can think of: a dance party. She puts her favorite song on her headphones, steps out from her counter, and awkwardly sways in place. It always takes her a little time to get into the groove, to forget that at any moment someone could look in her store and see her. Sophie doesn't care what people think . . . but sometimes it takes her a minute to remember that.

It doesn't take long before the music seeps into her bones and she has no choice but to close her eyes. Sophie is not a dancer, but that's never stopped her before. It probably should have, at least in public, she thinks, as she hears the door chime before she has time to pull her arms down and stop swaying her hips.

It's the guy, because *of course* it's the guy.

"Erm, hi," he says, as nervous as he appeared to be yesterday. But he's back, so good for him.

"Hi," she replies, stumbling over her own feet in a bid to stop moving. He looks at her like he knows she was just dancing around. As if he knows how embarrassed she feels. As if he knows she wishes the ground would swallow her whole. But he doesn't mention it.

"I was here yesterday, I needed—"

"The textbook," she answers for him, pulling her headphones from her ears and shoving her phone into her back pocket. She can still faintly hear the music.

"You remember?" he asks, stepping a little closer.

"It's barely been twenty-four hours." Honestly, even if she hadn't been thinking about him mere moments before he walked in, even if she hadn't been thinking about the pink of his lips when she reshelved the romance section, and even if she hadn't been thinking about the way his eyes flicked across her face when she applied her make up this morning, she still would have remembered him.

"Right." He laughs. "Sorry."

"Did you manage to get it from the library?" she asks, walking back behind her counter. She feels safe here.

"Ugh, no! And I went early today. I think someone took it out," he sighs.

"You're not allowed to take them out," she says, pulling her lip between her teeth.

"I know! Savages."

"Sorry." She winces. "I still don't sell it, though."

"Oh, I know. I was wondering if you knew anywhere that did. Or if you had any idea where I might even try to find one?"

"Um . . ." She thinks, wondering if she could bother her book club with something like this. She could even ask some of her old coursemates if they still have their textbooks, but she uses the word "mates" loosely, and she's pretty sure she saw them burning their books the second the term ended.

"Not like I expect you to have a super cool bookstore group chat or something," he says with a laugh.

"I can ask around," she says, "but I can't promise anything."

"That would be great, thank you so much," he exclaims, a little like he's expecting her to pull through with a very hard-to-get book two weeks away from exam season, even though she just told him she can't promise anything.

"Mm-hmm," she replies. She wants to say something else or for him to leave, because she can hear the music blaring from her headphones when they're silent, and he's close enough he can definitely hear it as well.

His eyes flick over her face and drop to her neck. It makes her feel hot for all the wrong reasons. She knows he's looking for the loud, peace-interrupting culprit that she's trying to smother in her jumper.

"One, please," he says, picking up a different bookmark from yesterday. Sophie's not even sure how he picked one he hasn't got already, because his gaze never drops from her face.

She rings him up, and he pulls out his phone. And if she spent the entire time she set up the card machine thinking about asking this borderline stranger for his number, even though she knows she's never going to ask him, that's her business.

"What, no tip today?" she asks, one brow high, as he dutifully opens a notebook from his bag and places the bookmark in with care. He laughs, looking up at her once before getting back to the task at hand.

"I didn't bring my wallet in the hopes of avoiding buying lunch when I packed a sandwich."

"How's that working out for you?" Sophie asks. It's a little after lunchtime, so his experiment should have its results by now.

"I ate my sandwich at eight minutes past nine this morning. I'm about to go back for afternoon lectures, and I hope my stomach is quieter than the music coming from your phone," he says with a dramatic almost feint against her bookshelf.

That's too bad. Sophie hates the thought of anyone being hungry, even if it's not for long. She reaches for the crisps she didn't eat earlier.

But wait—it takes her a second to register what he said. Her smile drops, and by the way he laughs, she's not being particularly sly about it.

"Oh, shut up!" she groans, throwing the bag of crisps at his chest. (It doesn't hit him—she doesn't have the best aim.) Her new curly-haired nemesis catches them easily, though, and his smile is so infectious that she rolls her eyes to stop from smiling back. It only partly works.

"For me?" he asks, his head cocked to the side.

"Even though I'm not sure you deserve them anymore," she grumbles.

"If I tell you I love Sean Paul, can I keep them?"

"Go away," she says, laughing, and finally pulls her phone from her pocket to mute the music.

"Your wish is my command," he replies. "Thank you for these."

She wants to say something cheesy about wanting him to stay, but she can't shuffle through her thoughts fast enough before he's at the door.

"You're welcome."

Chapter Three

Sophie cradles a cup of tea with both hands, holding the steaming drink millimeters from her face. It's cold. It's unreasonably cold, and she forgot to put the heating on a timer, so now she has to hope no one comes through the door to buy anything (even if that is the whole point of owning a shop) because her store needs at least forty-five minutes to warm up, and the second the door opens, the heat rushes out.

Every year, January tricks her. It's a bastard month for numerous reasons. Mainly because she pays herself early in December because she likes to leave present shopping to the last minute and then has to spend six weeks without a paycheck. (She has savings, but she loves a strict budget, and she's not some neanderthal who dips into them just because she saw a cute jumper in the sales.)

January is also always, without a doubt, warmer than she is expecting. When the low winter sun manages to warm her icy chin, it makes her think spring is right around the corner.

So she plants her forget-me-not seedlings and fills the pots on her small balcony at the back of her shop, and, more importantly, she starts waiting for the warmer weather. And then February hits, and she's never been colder a day in her life.

She knows that if she started her New Year's spring clean (that yes, she was supposed to start in January, but it has made its way onto—and been left unchecked on—every subsequent to-do list since), she would warm up, but it's the threat of those first few minutes when she thinks her fingers might fall off that keep her rooted to her seat.

She needs someone to come into the store. Then she'll *have* to move. So, she'll just wait for the perfect—

The door chimes before she's finished her thought. It's rude, because she really wasn't expecting it. But then *he* comes into sight—the guy from yesterday whose cute face plagued her thoughts while she cooked dinner—and suddenly, she's ten degrees hotter than she was a second ago.

"Hi again," he says with a small wave.

"Another bookmark for you?" Sophie asks.

His eyes flick to the mug from the other day. It's still in the same place, and it has nothing to do with her forgetting and everything to do with her wanting to hold on to the interaction. He won't know that, thankfully, but she still wishes she'd moved it, even if only so he thinks she's clean.

"Um, I got you this," he says, holding the gift bag in front of him. She doesn't take it, obviously. She has no idea who this guy is beyond the fact he has a nice voice and he's taller than her. "It's a mug," he says, lowering his arm slightly. He reaches into the bag and pulls out a large cream mug with a pastel pink smattering of small flowers. Forget-me-nots, if she had to guess. It makes her feel a little wild.

It's pretty.

"For me?"

"Yeah, well, because I threw my dirty change into yours the other day, and I felt awful about it when I was thinking about the whole thing yesterday evening—"

"You know I can just wash this one?"

"Yes," he says with a smile, "but you haven't."

"I was busy," she replies. It's not a lie. Her to-do list shows that she does, in fact, have other things to do. He smiles so brightly at her she feels a little lightheaded. He seems to think she's lying. She's not sure she likes him at all.

"Of course," he replies, pursing his lips as he nods. "Would you take this one anyway? I wouldn't expect you to use it—I could be some master criminal—but you could put tips in it instead of in the ones you like to drink from."

"You know tips aren't a thing in bookshops, right? It would just be a pretty, empty mug."

"You think it's pretty?"

"Of course," she says, with a shrug. "Forget-me-nots are my favorites."

"I took a guess," he replies. "I thought maybe your favorite bookmark was the pink one I bought yesterday, but I had nothing to base that on. Although, now I guess I might have been right all along?"

"Maybe, maybe not."

"Mm-hmm, okay." He laughs. "Can I buy this one, then?"

He places down a bookmark with a light pink background and darker pink roses. It's not the one she dislikes the most, but if she had to rank them, it wouldn't make the top ten. She won't tell him that, either.

"Sure." She wraps the bookmark in tissue paper, much as she did the day before. He hands her a five-pound note this time, and she enjoys the fact she'll get to touch his hand as she counts his change.

It seems like a routine now, as if she should expect him to come back tomorrow, and the next day. She's not sure what she's going to do when she runs out of days. The question is out of her mouth before she can think of a reason for it not to be.

"Are you coming to buy another one tomorrow?"

There are numerous reasons for her not to have asked. It's embarrassing. Now, if he comes back, it'll only be because she asked. So embarrassing.

"Of course. I need the full collection," he says, like that's obvious. It makes her smile.

"You could get the whole collection right now . . ." She shrugs.

"I could," he replies, his gaze staying on her face a beat too long. She looks at the counter, but her resolve barely lasts a second before she's looking at his face again. There's a clink and some shuffling, but her eyes are trained on his face, so if he's robbing her, well, that's just bad luck.

"See you tomorrow," he says, and walks away.

She barely mutters a "bye" before the door closes behind him. When she takes a breath, her eyes drop to the counter again and she sees the new mug next to her till.

It has his change in it.

Chapter Four

You see, this is why Sophie shouldn't have asked if curly hair was coming back into the store, because now it's hit three p.m. and he's nowhere to be seen. Now she's the fool.

She did see him walk toward the door, but then he left before it even creaked open. She doesn't *care*, obviously. But she does ask her mom if she's free that evening, because she misses her and she fancies a pizza and ice cream and maybe a movie. Also, her mom's place feels like home because it is, even though she moved out three years ago. Her mom's house, with the little front garden full of flowers and the overly colorful blankets and the quotes on the walls. That's her home.

Sophie lets herself into her mom's place at seven minutes past five, and her mom asks her to grab a spoon on her way through. The ice cream is already on the table, and the TV is paused at the beginning of *Legally Blonde*. Perfect.

"Wanna talk about it?" her mom asks, sharing her blanket when Sophie sits a little too close to her on the couch.

"No," Sophie grumbles. "I want to watch Warner be humiliated."

"Say no more," her mom says with a flick of the remote.

Her mom is the only person in the world who Sophie will let her guard down for, and that's probably because her mom waits until she's ready—she doesn't force anything.

"Did someone steal something?" her mom asks as Sophie brushes away a stray tear and the new law graduates throw their caps in the air. (There's something about "We did it!" that gets her every time.)

Sophie wants to say something like *my heart*, but she thinks her mom would have a heart attack, and she thinks she might be sick herself, so she doesn't.

"Nah, just a grumpy day," she replies, leaning closer to her mom on the couch. It's not a lie—not really—but it sits uncomfortably in her chest anyway.

"Mm-hmm," her mom replies. "*Easy A* time?"

"Absolutely," Sophie says. It's one of her favorite movies. A criminally underrated romcom, if she says so herself. A girl who has one friend, who isn't forced to pretend she's not pretty just because she has bushy eyebrows and glasses, who does some things that are questionable (if not hilarious, apart from the whole splitting-up-a-marriage thing) and still lands a guy who genuinely likes her and she trusts enough before they even kiss to tell him everything she's ever done wrong.

Sophie never lets anyone else that close. Some people (her mom, her therapist, her oldest friend she speaks to every six months and they catch up like no time has ever passed) suggest it's because she was always a "daddy's girl" growing up and he up and left in the middle of the night because he had another family.

But she likes being a recluse, she likes having things that she doesn't share with anyone, and she likes enjoying her own company. And she's not about to give the credit for the majority of her personality to a man who can't even be bothered to send a happy birthday text on the right day.

Her personality is not about him. It's hers.

Still, Sophie had a handful of friends growing up. Tabitha, who let Sophie borrow her coloring pencils; Graham, who was basically a little old man; and Chloe, who came to her house after school for dinner. They all had to go to separate secondary schools, and it was the worst day of her life (at the time, obviously—worse things have happened since—but she was utterly heartbroken and cried in front of three different people that day).

So, Sophie was over having friends. She never got close to anyone in senior school. (She didn't like the other loners because they were too dark and morbid, and she does like being alone, but also, the color pink is great.) She didn't mean to avoid people during university, but her mom got sick and she had to live at home to help her and do her coursework at the same time. She just didn't have time for friends.

Lucy didn't care that she was busy. Lucy is her one friend. Her best friend, if the obnoxious key chain Lucy forced Sophie to put on her keys is anything to go by. Sophie met Lucy during a volunteering session at the food bank that Sophie's mom dragged her along to (though Sophie actually enjoyed it and volunteered for four years before they moved). Lucy didn't care that Sophie didn't want to be friends—she was determined to be one anyway.

Lucy doesn't live nearby, and she has a baby (she's three and her middle name is Sophie and no, Sophie can't think about it without wanting to cry, so she stops) and their friendship thrives off little to no contact until one of them has a big life update, or they fancy a mani-pedi they'd drive three hours for. Sophie usually only goes for the baby cuddles, because she doesn't like people touching her, but it's worth it all the same.

So, Sophie has always liked to be alone. But as she watches *the* scene, *the* reveal, *the* confession of love, she wonders if it would be all that bad to let someone in.

Chapter Five

February the twenty-sixth is the worst day in the history of worst days. First, Sophie's alarm doesn't go off (or she forgot to put it on after staying up too late reading a book, but whatever). Then, she brushes her teeth with the toothpaste she doesn't like but refuses to throw out because that's wasteful and she'd rather just ignore the tube on the sink and reach for the minty one that foams. Then her mascara wand pokes her in the eye, and she trips over her own foot in a rush to get out the door.

She doesn't have time to sit with her cup of tea and overthink this month's book orders she hasn't unpacked yet, or the radiator she needs to get fixed in the back office, or the part-time sales assistant she should really hire sometime soon, or the way curly-hair looked in his green sweater two days ago, or the fact that he didn't stop by yesterday. And the sky is so dark it may as well be midnight even though it's barely the afternoon. So, no, Sophie is not having a good day.

Sure, now she's in her store and she's made her way through six tasks on her to-do list, her mood could have improved, but she prefers to let things fester and ruin her entire day rather than admit defeat. She's not a quitter. Besides, she works better when she's concentrating, and it still counts as concentration, even if she's focused on the wrong things.

Still, she ticks off "completing orders" and tries not to smother her smile as the door chimes sound. She's not sure if she's conditioned herself to be a little happier whenever the door opens because usually that means someone wants to talk about books, or look at books, or purchase books, or if it's the fact she won't be alone with her own thoughts anymore. Sophie chooses to believe it's the latter and that she hasn't actually made herself Pavlov's dog, because that's far too upsetting for a Wednesday morning. The thought shoves her moodiness further into her head.

Her mood increases tenfold when she glances up and sees the curly hair—the hair that invades her thoughts when she's not even thinking—walking toward her. But she can't have that, because she's not the lead in a romance book, and she's not even sure she would ever want to be. So she shoves her smile back down.

"What's up, sunshine?" he says.

"Sunshine?" she grumbles.

"Hmm . . . what's up, storm cloud?" he asks as she pouts at her to-do list. She rolls her eyes and lets a small smile slide onto her face, because she thinks if she tries to clamp it down, she might break her jaw.

"Are you planning on naming every weather phenomenon?" Sophie asks.

"Only the ones that start with an *S*."

"Mm-hmm," she replies. "Something for class?"

"Maybe." The lie is obvious on his face as he bends to look over her bookmarks for the umpteenth time, but she lets him get away with it because she doesn't know how to make her brain work properly when he looks up at her from under his lashes.

"Why didn't you come in yesterday?" Sophie asks. It's supposed to come out all nonchalant, like she doesn't really care why he half walked into the store only to then leave, but she thinks it sounds a little desperate. She's not sure, though, so if he asks her, she can deny it.

"Oh, you saw that." He laughs and runs his hand through his hair. As if she wouldn't find him anywhere. As if that's not something she should be embarrassed by considering she doesn't even know his name. His hair is straighter today than usual. She prefers it curly.

"I forgot my wallet, and my phone died because Millie was playing on it in the morning. I need to be your favorite customer, but how can I do that without buying something?" he asks with a small shrug.

Millie. She files that name to the back of her mind.

"I'd give you an IOU," she replies. She only gives IOUs to Tyler—a fifteen-year-old menace she used to babysit when he was a chubby baby that tried to pull all her hair out—and honestly, that might the thing that bankrupts her. She refuses to tell curly hair he'd be her favorite customer without buying anything. His face lights up like maybe this admission was too much.

"You would?"

"Calm down, dork," she says with a laugh, pushing her hair behind her shoulder. Suddenly, she feels a little too hot. "You're in here all the time. It's not like you'd get away with not paying me three ninety-nine."

"Do you mind?" he asks. She knows what he's asking, and she knows she can't get away with not answering it, but she's not sure she's comfortable giving out that information yet. It's scary.

"Do I mind what?" Sophie asks, swallowing as he smiles at her.

"That I come here a lot."

"It's not the worst part of my day," she mutters.

"Okay, calm down, don't flatter me too much!"

"You're so annoying," she groans, throwing her head back as he laughs. She likes it when he laughs. She wonders if she could make the sound her ringtone.

"Do you make these?" he asks, running his thumb over the matte finish of the bookmark. He's asking a lot of questions today, but even though she didn't sleep well, she doesn't mind.

"Yes," she replies without thinking. The answer feels uncomfortable in the air, her throat getting tight with the admission, but he seems none the wiser. He looks at the *S* in the corner longer than she'd like, but if he asked her name right now, she'd tell him.

"You're crazy talented," he says.

"Thank you." Her mom always taught her to accept praise where it's deserved—that saying "no I'm not" when someone compliments you on something you worked hard on is doing yourself, and them, a disservice.

"You're welcome."

She wonders what he's planning on doing with them. Maybe he buys them and gives them to girls he sleeps with because he's twisted and thinks it's funny. Maybe they're all screwed up at the bottom of his bag. Maybe they don't even make it to his house—maybe they're in the bin the second he leaves.

Maybe Millie keeps them.

But it's nothing that she's going to ask today.

Chapter Six

"This one today, please, storm cloud," he states, standing up and placing the black bookmark with white tulips on the counter.

"You don't have to keep buying bookmarks," she says. She doesn't tell him he'd be her favorite customer even if he never stepped foot in her store again.

"I know, but they're pretty, and I need to finish my collection . . . *and* I know I've been your favorite customer since the first day, but I need you to maybe, possibly, if you want, break your no-lying rule and tell me I'll pass this exam even though I haven't been able to get the book from the library." He grimaces.

Sophie looks at him, at his hopeful brown eyes and his cute fluffy eyebrows, and she thinks, *fine,* she would maybe, possibly, bend her rules for him, but that's not something she wants to admit to him or to herself right now.

Thankfully, it won't be a lie. She bends behind the counter, grabs the chemistry textbook that came in this morning, and places it beside the till.

"You won't fail."

"Oh my God! You do have the book?! I thought you didn't sell them!"

"I don't. I ordered it for you." The way his face shines suggests she should have just admitted to the lying thing.

"Just for me?" he asks, a small smirk on his face that she wants to kiss away.

Yes, just for him. She scoured the internet and messaged contacts in her bookshop community, and she even had to agree to go to a networking event next month, and she probably spent more time looking for the book than she did reading anything this past week—but she found it.

And the way her heart thumps at the look on his face suggests she'd do it all again in a heartbeat. How utterly embarrassing.

"Go away," she grumbles, her fingers tapping on the cover.

"You don't want me to fail!" he sings, pointing to the textbook she's still holding down on the counter.

"You're so annoying." She laughs, but he forces his face into something serious. It doesn't work, but she humors him anyway.

"Storm cloud," he says, though it sounds like a question.

"Curly," she replies. It's mortifying, because yes, she does think about him enough to have formulated something in her head to call him, because he's apparently refusing to tell her his name, even though she's never asked him, and every name she can think of doesn't suit him.

"Curly?"

"I'm choosing to ignore that I said that." It's embarrassing, and she almost immediately regrets it, but he looks so delighted she can't find it in herself to do anything other than laugh.

He laughs with her, and she wonders if she should let him take the book away and trust that he will bring it back. She doesn't want him to leave. She's just not sure how to ask him to stay.

"So . . . how much do you know about chemistry?"

"I took the class five years ago." Sophie shrugs. It's the most information she's given to anyone outside of her family since she was in high school, and she told her project partner she wasn't feeling well. It's daunting in a way it shouldn't be, because she only told him something small, borderline insignificant—not her credit card number—but there's a voice in the back of her head calling her an idiot.

Still, she expects him to be excited that they share a similar interest, even if her master's degree is nothing more than an expensive piece of paper she doesn't even have in a frame now that she owns a bookshop.

That's not what he talks about.

"So, you're like, erm . . . twenty-seven?" he asks.

"Yep," she says, her lips popping.

"Same." He smiles, and a handsome blush covers his cheeks. *Phew*. He's not as young as she thought.

"Cool."

"Cool."

It's awkward in a good way when he looks at her for a beat too long, and she bites her lip as she takes a shaky breath.

"So . . ." She doesn't know what to say next, so she stands there, tapping her fingers against the shiny cover of the textbook.

"How busy is the shop usually on a Thursday morning in late February?" he asks, his hands tight against his backpack strap.

"Not very," Sophie replies a little too fast, her eyes flicking over his face. It's not a lie. It's not the truth, either. The bookshop picks and chooses when to be busy, and there's every chance she'll get a million customers before the end of the day.

"So, if I went to get us some food, would you want to keep me company while I work through the chapters?" he asks, his brows so high she's surprised they don't get lost in his hair.

"If you get me some sour sweets, I might even help you," she says.

"Yeah?" He beams, rocking back and forth on his heels.

"Yeah," she replies, pushing some hair behind her ear and wondering if she has time to run to her apartment upstairs and throw on some perfume and check her makeup. He wouldn't notice, right?

"Okay. So, sour sweets and coffee? Hmm, no—tea?" he asks.

"Tea is great, thanks." She doesn't tell him how she likes her tea, because that information seems even more important than her credit card information, and she's already told him her educational background and how old she is.

"Okay, I'll be right back," he says, walking backward, avoiding the table of books somehow. She watches him go, trying to stifle her grin when he lingers near the door. She doesn't blame him; it's Baltic outside.

"Erm, what name should I put on your tea?" he asks, his hand against the door.

She thinks about it as she looks at the outline of his shoulders, the straight line of his nose that she's desperate to sketch while he's gone, and the curl of his hair. The upturn of his lips, and the thickness of his thighs. She might even legally change her name to storm cloud because that's how much she likes how it sounds on his tongue.

"Sophie," she says.

"Sophie," he repeats with a smile she wants to pin on her jacket.

"I'm Lukas."

Chapter Seven

The mornings get a little brighter as February fades into March. It's one of her favorite months of the year. The weather doesn't have the same bite to it anymore, and she can hang her washing out to dry on the line (but only when she drops by her mom's house, because Sophie doesn't have a garden, and hanging her washing outside above the back of the bookshop doesn't seem like a great idea). Luckily for her, her mom lives two streets down and has a massive garden.

Sophie hangs her clothes on the line and faux grumbles at her mom when she finds some of her clothes in there as well. Sophie doesn't mind, not really.

It's always been her and her mom for as long as she can remember. There are photos of other people, her father, and grandparents, but everyone else is gone. Some through the inevitable aging process, and others through choice.

"Do you reckon March or April for the onions?" her mom shouts from the table at the top of the garden. Sophie hangs a jumper up, making sure not to stretch it out, before she walks back to the table to answer.

Twice a year, Sophie and her mom update their growing calendar. They try to plant as many flowers as they can in her mom's garden because she thinks they smell pretty (true) and they look nice (also true), and because her mom can't get out as much as she'd like. So they make her garden into her own oasis. Sometimes, they try to plant vegetables, but it's only semi-successful.

"Um, well, we planted some back in January. How are they doing?"

"I did forget to water them for a little bit . . ." her mom states with a wave of her hand.

"How long is 'a bit'?" Sophie asks, wrapping a blanket over her mom's shoulders. It's warmer, but it's not *warm*.

"Ever?"

"Mom," Sophie groans, adding another round of sweet peas to the calendar.

"Uh-huh," her mom replies. "How's the store?"

"It's going good."

"Have you hired anyone else yet?"

"Ugh, I should. I've half written the advert, I just . . . you know."

"I know," her mom says, "but if you never take the risk, how will you know if it would have worked out?"

Sophie can feel her mom's eyes boring into her skull. Sophie knows if she looks up at her mom now, she'll tell her everything, and she doesn't want to do that because then she'll have to explain how nervous she is and her mom will say something cheesy.

"It's just a Saturday job, mom," Sophie mutters, writing the plants down that she planted for her mom months ago but knows are dead without her having to ask.

"Mm-hmm. That goes for other things as well, you know."

Sophie knows her mom knows something is up because she knows her better than anyone in the world. She just doesn't know how to explain that maybe there might be someone else she wants to know her that well, someone that understands how she feels without her having to explain it all in painstaking detail. Maybe she needs her mom's cheesy advice . . . just this once.

"I know," Sophie whispers, "but what if I fall?"

"Oh, my darling," her mom exclaims, always far too happy to be given the chance to recite a quote that could be found on any wooden plaque in any decor store (and almost definitely in her mother's guest toilet). "But what if you fly?"

"Alright," Sophie groans. That was a lot, even for her. If she tells her mom, then it feels real, and she's not even sure what she's feeling yet. But then her mom smiles—a small thing, as she notes down the next seeds they're going to buy at the garden center—and Sophie's never been able to keep anything from her.

"There's a guy," Sophie says.

Her mom drops her pen. (It's as dramatic as it sounds.)

"Tell. Me. Everything."

Chapter Eight

Sophie can't tell if she's more disappointed in herself for being excited at the thought of seeing Lukas again, or if she's more disappointed that she hasn't been on a date in so long she may have mistaken his being friendly for flirtation.

It's whatever.

(It's definitely the fact she told her mom and now she either has to tell her she was wrong, or she'll have to avoid her for the next three months while she forgets about him.)

It's been a week since she bought him the book. A week since she helped him pass the exam. (She hasn't seen his score due to his disappearing act, but she knows he passed.) A full week, and he hasn't been back in the shop since. She figures he won't have another exam that he'd need her textbooks for, so why else would he come back? He said he didn't have much time to read, so she's not sure what she thought he would come back into her bookshop for. But he came in before, and that's the most annoying thing about it.

She tries not to think too hard about it or she'll think about how he clearly doesn't mind her body, with the way his gaze lingered on her hips when she grabbed another notepad. He might be one of the guys that put up with her because he likes her face—with the many times he looked at her lips she'd wager at least five bookmarks on it—but there's something about her he doesn't like in the way she likes him.

So he doesn't think about her when she's not around, and he doesn't think about the ways he wanted to kiss her, and he doesn't dream about introducing her to his family.

Not that she *likes him*, likes him. Ugh. She feels like a lovestruck teenager, and it's humiliating, and also the best feeling in the world. It's silly, really. They only hung out for like six hours, and a couple of random minutes on other days, but it was effortless in a way it never has been before.

Now, Sophie spends most of her days getting actual work done. Work she'd neglected when Lukas was here. It's an embarrassing amount, if she's honest. So, she starts her new to-do list. What she really needs to do is hire someone else. Probably just for the weekend, for now. She's nervous to take someone on full-time in case there's a recession, or she drops dead, or eight new bookshops open on her road and she has to let them go.

But instead, she sketches some new bookmarks that she'll probably never print, and she allows herself another sixteen minutes to wallow, because she likes to start new activities on the hour. She chooses a color palette that looks a little too much like the color of his jumper and the blush on his cheeks, and she slams her sketchbook closed because she feels awful about how this bookmark would become her new favorite and she doesn't want it to be associated with him.

She's known for her dramatics. They're annoying. (She'll blame those on her dad.)

So she thinks about how she liked him being around, how she liked talking to someone new, and she missed the feeling of thinking about someone in that way. Like imagining your life with someone you just met, what they'd be like grocery shopping, whether they'd fold laundry as it came out of the dryer or if they'd wait until they got home. She misses the feeling of being with someone, even in the limited way they were.

She misses the terrifying ordeal of letting yourself be known by someone. But it's only been a week, and she knew him for a consecutive time of about twenty hours, so she should also get a grip. So, she's about to redownload a dating app that she knows she'll delete by the end of the evening because, *ew*, when the bell rings, and . . . *oh*.

There he is.

Sophie sits up a little straighter, schooling her face into something that attempts to be neutral. Lukas didn't say he was coming back. He didn't ask for her number. She didn't ask for his number, so she can't be mad. A little disappointed, maybe. Because he did look at her in a way that made her stomach flip, and he did creep closer to her for the six hours he was there, two of those past closing time, and he did keep passing her the green sour sweets because she said they were her favorite, even though she was within reaching distance the entire time.

"Hi," he says.

"Hi," she replies. She flips her sketchbook open, because she's not about to act a fool just because he turned up again. He could be here for any reason.

"How are you?" he asks, his hands by his side, his fingers tapping on the outsides of his thigh.

"Good, and you?"

"Mm-hmm, good, yep," he replies, his head bobbing. He stands a weird distance away from her, rocking on his heels. She can't decide if he's here for a book or for her. Maybe he has another project. She frowns, closing her book and sliding it to the end of the counter.

He grabs a book from the shelf without looking (it's a mistake, that's the self-help section) and takes it over.

"Can I buy this please?" he asks, refusing to look at her, and she thinks he's entirely too cute and she's still wildly confused.

"You want a book on 'how to appear normal at social events'?"

He blushes the deepest shade of pink she's seen, and she feels like she's in a Jane Austen novel. Like if he touched her hand right now, she might combust on the spot. She's not in a Jane Austen novel—she does realize that—but it's always nice to think about it, even if she doesn't actively want it.

"Are you—"

"Could I have come back to see you the next day?" he rushes out. It takes her by surprise, and she's not sure how well she hides it, with the small smile that graces his face.

"Did you want to?" she asks, her eyes tracking every movement on his face in case there's something that suggests he's lying.

"Yes," he says definitively.

Sophie doesn't want to be waiting on people. She doesn't like the idea of placing her happiness in someone else's hands—even if it's only a tad.

It's different with Lukas. She kind of wants to sit with him in silence, and she wants to tell him everything, even though she can barely entertain the thoughts in her own mind for longer than a few minutes. She wants to know what his face will look like when she tells him she graduated top of her class only to ignore her degree anyway. She wants to know how he'll react if she told him she doesn't really like peanut butter that much.

"Then, yes," she says, tucking a strand of hair behind her ear.

"Cool, that's—cool," he replies. He grabs another bookmark, and she rings him up. He hands her twenty pounds, shoving the change back in the mug he bought her by the cash register because it reminded her of him on the long seven days when she wished she had his number. Maybe she should ask for it now.

"Alright, bye."

"What?" she says, laughing lightly, but it's too late. He's already out the door, and she couldn't be more confused if she tried.

Chapter Nine

Sophie finds herself smiling through the tasks on her to-do list that usually make her want to crawl into a ball on the floor. She breaks down the cardboard boxes from the orders and throws them in the recycling bin, with its heavy lid, outside. She walks with a bounce in her step (though it wouldn't be noticeable to the human eye—she thinks she probably still looks like she'd want to kill someone if they looked at her) as she restocks the toilet rolls in the bathroom. She hums as she peels reduction stickers off books that didn't sell, even though they always ball up and she gets the residue on her nails. (She doesn't try to sell them again, but she will drop them at the charity shop later.)

She even takes her phone out and snaps a quick ridiculous selfie with her peony bookmark to send to Lucy. (She designed it because Lucy sent her peonies one summer when she had to go back home and Sophie was upset about it.)

She still has a to-do list that's too long to complete, and she's still a little confused at how quickly Lukas left, but the fact he turned up at all brings a smile to her face that just won't leave.

Lukas doesn't let her be confused for too long. He comes back into the shop about fifteen minutes later, after she's just checked off the orders from her to-do list. A string of customers came through the door for their orders, and once again, Sophie's mind is occupied with running a bookstore, so she's happy to see him. (She really should do the ad for a vacancy. It's on the list for sure.)

"Hi," she says, unable to keep her excitement that he returned from her voice.

"Hi," he replies, bounding over. He places a tea on her counter, and it smells how she expects him to taste. Sweet and a little too hot. Not that that's something she's thought about at length . . . But she does enjoy that he likes to drink tea during the day. She thinks even a whiff of coffee in the afternoon would keep her up at night. Lukas looks at her expectantly, and she shuffles under his gaze.

"Oh," he says with a light laugh, reaching to spin the cup until she can see her name written on the label.

"For me?" she asks uselessly. Of course it's for her.

"It's to make up for not coming back. Not that you were waiting for me—I wasn't, I didn't mean it like that, I just meant that *I* was waiting to come back, and I could have because I found any excuse to come and see you before, so I don't know why knowing your name freaked me out, and I didn't know if you—"

"Lukas." She laughs, letting him off the hook as a shiver runs through her with how warm the cup is against her palms. "Thanks for the tea."

"Yeah, of course," he replies. He rubs his lips together, and she likes it when he's a little nervous because it makes her heart stutter knowing he's in the same position as her. She shouldn't like him this much, but she really can't help it.

"So, erm—"

"Do you want to stay?" she asks, and he lets out a breath as he throws his bag to the floor.

"Does Popeye eat lettuce?" he asks, his brows high.

"No."

"Oh, wait—what does he eat?"

"Spinach."

"Well, in that case—"

"Don't say it again." Sophie laughs as Lukas walks closer. "That's the worst joke I've ever heard."

"Doesn't matter," he says with a smile. "It made you laugh."

Chapter Ten

Whenever Lukas comes into the shop (always before two thirty, but she'll take the time to figure that out later) he doesn't sit down much. Rather, he wanders around the store asking her things about the books he pulls from the shelves. She finds she doesn't mind telling him.

Sometimes.

Sometimes, he asks her a specific question about a character in a book she always dreamed someone would ask her about, but she's overanalyzed the book so much that it feels too personal to share it with anyone else. Besides, why would Lukas care that she thinks *Clueless* is one of the best modern-day adaptations of Shakespeare?

Sophie blushes deeply, so much so that she thinks the low light of the bookstore and the darker hue of her skin mean nothing when Lukas hums an agreement to a statement she made. He'd be able to see it from space. But he's not looking at her. He's writing notes on his phone.

She asks him what he's writing, whether it's about the book or maybe he's noting down a recipe or something he forgot earlier. He blushes and tells her to go away, even though she's still sitting behind her counter and nowhere near him. It makes her heart feel all too full.

And so starts the beginning of her life with Lukas.

Sophie is good at making lunch for herself because she only lives upstairs and it would take longer for her to close the shop and run to the café down the street than it would for her to go and grab the ingredients to make a sandwich.

"Really?" Lukas asks, when his stomach grumbles for the third time that day.

"I don't mind." She shrugs. "I'll make myself one too."

"Like a picnic date?" he asks, looking over at her as he pulls another book off the shelves.

"You're adorable." She laughs as she moves to walk upstairs. "I don't have a picnic blanket, though."

"Thanks, Soph," he says, and the nickname flies out of his mouth so naturally she wants to catch it in her hands and file it in the folds of her heart.

"Don't burn my shop down," she says instead.

Sophie makes matching sandwiches because she thinks it's cute (and she didn't ask Lukas what he wanted). She grabs some crisps and a bottle of water and she does not check her hair in the bathroom mirror before she leaves. She mulls over whether he meant it was a *date* date or if that's just a saying. She hasn't come to a conclusion by the time she walks back downstairs.

When she gets back, she notices Lukas pottering around, tidying the store, and a customer leaving with a bag of books. Maybe she can't just run and make lunch because the guy she likes is hungry. She decides she'll make the advert for a Saturday position after lunch. She might even ask Lukas for his advice.

She places the sandwiches on the counter before going to flip the sign to closed. She'll only leave it for twenty minutes or so. It's so they don't have to handle books with breadcrumbs all over their hands, obviously.

When she turns around, she sees Lukas sitting on the red and orange blanket she uses in the winter to keep warm. The food is positioned in what she thinks *he thinks* is an artistic way (the sandwiches are free from her beeswax paper and the crisps are in a makeshift bowl) but she doesn't mind, not really.

He's placed her vase on the ground next to them with a bunch of flowers in it. They're yellow daffodils, and she thinks maybe this is the best lunch she's ever had.

Chapter Eleven

The low winter sun shines through the windows of the shop. It's bright, desperate for spring sunshine. It's beautiful and holds a touch of warmth if felt through the windows. It also shows just how dirty the glass is. So, Sophie grabs a bowl of hot, soapy water, puts her music on her phone, and gets to work on the stubborn dust and leftover fake snow from the holiday season.

It's a bonus that she can people-watch from here. She makes up various scenarios for the woman with a cane—maybe she's on her way to the park. And the man with three children trying to hold onto his hand—he's going to lunch.

Sophie is dancing sitting down. It's one of her favorite things to do, but she wishes she had someone here to do it with her.

A blonde lady with a pram passes by the window, and the glow from her hair reminds her of her best friend. She could call her right now and she'd join in on her party without needing any more information. Sophie reaches for her phone, but the bell rings instead. She is about to spin around to greet whoever dared interrupt her private concert, but a booming voice breaks through the music before she has a chance.

"I need a book on babies, stat!"

Sophie drops her sponge with a splash and soap suds lightly splash the closest bookshelf, but she doesn't mind—it won't ruin anything. Besides, nothing could bring her down right now.

"Lucy?!" she squeals. Lucy has texted her recently, and it's taken everything within Sophie not to tell her about Lukas. Because it's new. It's too new, and she's not even sure what it is—only what she knows she wants it to be.

"Oh my God," Lucy replies, her blue eyes squinting as she looks Sophie over. Her cheeks are the same pink as usual, but she's managing to look flawless instead of freezing cold, as everyone else looks outside.

"What?" Sophie asks, practically whining, but she thinks she saves it at the end.

"You *are* in love!"

"What?!" It's possible Sophie has never been that energetic in greeting her before. It's not her fault. She saves all her excitement for Annabelle and for when she's had more than three alcoholic drinks.

"Elaine said—"

"El—when did you talk to my mom?" Sophie asks, knowing full well they have a friendship beyond Sophie. Lucy basically lived with them through the latter half of university because Sophie couldn't cope by herself (not that she'd ever admit it) and because Lucy was lonely away from home (not that she wouldn't kill someone for saying the same thing).

"Oh, please, SJ," Lucy replies with a roll of her eyes. She pushes the pram further into the store, close enough Sophie can peer over the edge and see that Annabelle is awake.

"Hi, baby!" Sophie coos, reaching in to unbuckle her as Annabelle reaches for her.

"Don't change the subject," Lucy replies, taking Annabelle's coat from Sophie's hands so she can twist her in the air easier.

"You're the one who talks about me to my mother behind my back," Sophie says, while maintaining her smile battle with Annabelle.

"If you watched Grey's Anatomy with us, you'd be clued in to our conversations."

"You never even sent me the invite, and mom says her internet connection isn't good enough for three people on videochat and the ability to stream all at once."

"She's right," Lucy says. "Either way, who is he?"

"Oh my God, and here I was thinking you just missed me!" Sophie grumbles, popping Annabelle on her hip.

Lucy's gaze softens, her beautiful closed-mouth smile taking over her face.

"I always miss you. Who is he?"

"I don't know why you're asking like my mom didn't give you all the information already," Sophie replies.

"I wanna hear it from you, ya grump. Please?"

Lucy gives her best pleading face, smiling as she bats her eyelashes. Sophie sighs, but she feels better with Annabelle leaning against her.

"His name is Lukas . . ."

Chapter Twelve

Sophie isn't mad that Lukas wasn't around when Lucy came in. Not because she thinks they wouldn't get on—she thinks they wouldn't even need her to have a conversation, they'd find a million other things to talk about—but because there would be pressure there. If Lukas showed any suggestion he didn't like Lucy, or Annabelle, well, she'd never be able to see him again. And if Lucy thought something was off with Lukas, she'd have to seriously consider that she might be right, and everything in her doesn't want that at all.

So, she's not mad.

It's been a week since he came back for no reason, and he's come to see her every day since. He always comes with tea, and sometimes he brings a doughnut, too, depending on the time of day. He often runs out quickly (when it gets a little too close to three o'clock) but she doesn't mind because he looks cute when he's flustered, and she thinks he'll tell her where he goes at some point.

Today, the doorbell chimes as she finishes ringing up a customer, and she forgets to hide her smile when he skips down the aisle. His hands are behind his back, and she waits for the door to close, leaving them alone, before she outwardly acknowledges his existence.

"Hi, Lukas."

"You're so rude to me, Soph," he grumbles. "I know you saw me."

"Did not."

"Mm-hmm. So your cheeks aren't pink because you're excited to see me, and you're pretending you're not because you're usually moody on a Monday?"

The fact he observes her enough to figure these things out so quickly should petrify her, because once someone knows you, they know all the ways to destroy you. But she trusts Lukas, even if she shouldn't.

"Why are you so obsessed with me?" she says, frowning as he beams at her and walks closer. She's desperate to touch him, to see if his arms are as firm as she thinks, to see if his hair is soft and if his nose is cold to the touch because it's always pink.

"I can't help it, storm cloud." He laughs, his hand coming from behind his back to rest across his forehead like he's a widow in an old movie. The hand that is up holds a bunch of flowers—white tulips covered with a little dew.

Sophie clamps her lip down at the fact he listened to her rant about her favorite flowers the other day and the fact he hasn't seemed to notice that they're out in the open. She thinks it's dangerous the way she likes him, because good things never last, so if she were sensible, she'd pull back.

"Are those for me?" she asks, and his eyes widen. She tries to hold back a little giggle, but it doesn't work.

"Oh, fuck."

If she were sensible, she wouldn't let herself fall in love.

"What if I said they weren't?" he asks, though his arm is reaching out to her already.

"That would be alright." She shrugs. She's lying. Sort of.

Thankfully, he doesn't know that.

Lukas gasps, practically recoiling as he does.

"I can't believe you broke your no-lying rule for flowers but not when my joke wasn't funny!"

"Oh my God," she says with a laugh. "You're the worst."

"I'm your favorite, Soph," he replies with a roll of his eyes. "But they are for you."

"Yeah?" she whispers, her hands wrapped around the stems. They're beautiful, and she wants to say as much, but her throat feels tight and her eyes feel wet.

"Yeah," he replies, placing his bag behind the counter like he's staying for a while. "Just for you."

Sophie places the tulips in water and a vase she had to run upstairs to find. She wonders if it's reasonable to leave them in the shop and then take them to her apartment for the evening.

Lukas is wrapping an order for someone when she gets back. She wants to walk up behind him and wrap her arms around his waist. She wants to rest her forehead in the space between his shoulder blades. She wants to see if he's comfy, even if everything she's seen through his jumpers suggests otherwise.

Instead, she places the vase on the counter and fiddles with a few of the stems, because Lukas turned to face her and she doesn't want to look at him right now.

"Stop ignoring me," he says, nudging her gently with his arm.

"I'm doing no such thing, Luke."

"Oh, Luke, is it?"

"Shut up," she groans.

Lukas mimes zipping his lips closed as he moves to wander around the store. Sophie misses his voice already.

"Lucy is in town," she says. It's been silent for eight minutes. A nice silence, a happy silence. But the sentence just flew out of her like she needed to tell him right now.

"Who's that?" he asks. He's looking at the "new in" section, and she can tell something's off. She's wanted to change it around for a few weeks, but she can't figure out how to improve it, only how to move it slightly.

"She's my best friend."

"Yeah?"

"Mm-hmm," she replies. That's probably enough information for right now. She moves out from behind the counter, ready to organize the crime section.

"Where did you meet?"

Hell. She likes to tell him things because he sounds so excited when she does. It's the worst.

"Um—"

"You don't have to tell me just because I asked," he replies.

"I want to tell you," she mutters, refusing to turn around to face him, instead fiddling with two identical books. "I'm just not very good at it."

"I don't think that's true. But you never lie, so . . ." She can feel him walking closer to her, and whenever he's nearby, she loses all sense of decorum and wants to climb him like a tree. His hands fall against the small of her waist, his fingertips grazing her ribs.

"I've got an idea for the 'new in' section. Can I show you?" he asks, his lips pressed against the back of her head.

"I can't believe you want to change my store around," she jokes. It doesn't land, because her voice is too breathy, but he lets her get away with it.

"As if this hasn't been driving you mad, Soph," he says, laughing as he spins her around. She leans just slightly, the back of her head resting against his shoulder, and closes her eyes.

"Okay," she says. "Tell me."

She listens to him with her eyes closed because it makes things easier to imagine. Or because she feels comfier than she has in years, leaning against him as he whispers his thoughts in her ear. She thinks maybe she wants to hear everything like this from now on.

"What do you think?" he asks, his arms fully wrapped around her waist.

"It's a great idea," she replies. She can't do it right now because she's got to get ready for dinner with Lucy, but she wonders if he'd want to help her. She could ask him . . . or she could wait to do it until he shows up in the shop next because she's a baby who can't ask someone for help.

"I told you, storm cloud," he whispers, his lips grazing her ear, "the customer is always right."

"You're so—" She pushes away from him, but he doesn't let her move very far.

"Your favorite customer?!" he jokes.

"Mm-hmm, you're my favorite," she says.

"Can I get that in writing?" he asks, spinning her around to face him again. She rolls her eyes at him, but she'll write it down if he asks.

Sophie thinks it's a cosmic injustice that one of the only times she gets to see Lukas in the dark evening light, she has other plans. She likes the way his hair shines in the store lights, and she likes the way his eyes sparkle under the streetlights. She wishes she got to see it more.

"You need to go, right?" he asks.

"Um . . ." She hasn't actually told him about her dinner plans because she doesn't want him to think she's inviting him. She's not, even if she'd like to go for dinner with him. She wants to do that alone so her nervous energy is just shared with him and not with her best friend, who will pick up on everything she wants to say but doesn't.

"It's okay." He shrugs, and his eyes flick to her lips just once before he pulls back. "I'll see you tomorrow."

Lukas waits for her to lock up before he leaves.

"University," she says as she locks the door. He knows she lives upstairs (not that she's gathered the courage to ask him up yet), but he waits for her light to turn on before he leaves. He doesn't tell her that, but she likes to sneak a look out of her curtain.

"Hmm?" he asks as he fiddles with his headphones, trying to untie the lead just by shaking them around.

"That's where I met Lucy."

He smiles, and it makes the snakes in her chest wriggle around. Sophie pulls her bottom lip between her teeth, but her smile matches his.

Chapter Thirteen

"I miss Annabelle," Sophie moans, linking her arm tightly with Lucy's. It's bloody freezing, but they decided walking back to her place was the best idea after all the food they ate.

"Wow, are you even friends with me for me?" Lucy laughs, the effects of the bottle of wine they shared evident in her tone.

"You're a perk of my relationship with Annabelle, honestly."

"Ha!"

"I know you're leaving tomorrow," Sophie starts, "but when are you coming back?"

"Oh, needy! Well, not to get you too excited . . ."

"Oh my God," Sophie says, stopping in place as she watches Lukas come to a stop at a traffic light on the other side of the road. Lucy follows her line of sight and gasps as she shakes next to her.

"That's him, isn't it?" Lucy asks, her voice giddy with excitement. Honestly, she's the worst.

"Maybe . . ."

"It is!"

"How would you know that? Maybe I'm trying to wind you up," Sophie replies, as Lukas presses the button to cross the road. He hasn't seen them yet, and she's not sure she wants him to. She's never seen him outside the store. Well, she's seen him on the pavement outside, so she knows how his nose gets pink in the cold, and how his hair moves in the strong wind.

He's never seen her outside of the shop, though. He's never seen her with her hair blowing in the wind, or with her scarf threatening to blow away because she decided to just throw it over her shoulders after dinner instead of looping it around her neck. He's never seen her outside of her cozy jumpers and leggings.

But she dressed up (slightly—they only went for dinner, she's not going to the Oscars) and she made an effort outside of daylight, and now there's a swooping in her gut at the thought that maybe he won't like what he sees.

"Oh, *please*, SJ. You hate lying, and your 'maybe' is just a 'yes but please don't ask again,' but it's me, so obviously, I'm going to ask again. Is that him?"

"You're so—yes, it's him."

"Ah, very cute. Do you want to walk past?" Lucy asks. If there's anything Sophie loves about Lucy, it's her inability to embarrass people. You don't want to drink anymore during a drinking game? Lucy would never pressure you. Someone is trying to make a joke at your expense? Lucy will pretend she doesn't understand it and change the conversation. You want to walk straight past a guy you like because you're not ready to introduce him to anyone when you barely know what you'd introduce him as? She'll walk you past.

"I—"

"Sophie!" Lukas calls out with a wave. Well. He isn't as attuned to her inner turmoil as Lucy, but that's okay.

"Say the word and I'll pick you up and run," Lucy whispers.

"Hey," he says again when he's in front of her. They've moved to the side of the pavement because they're not rude, and apparently this might take longer than five seconds of pleasantries.

"Hey," Sophie replies, her throat feeling dry as she takes a deep breath. She watches him flick his gaze to Lucy as if he might be expecting an introduction, but he doesn't know she's useless at this. That she's only ever introduced Lucy to one guy before and that ended about twenty minutes after the fact.

"Lucy, right?" Lukas asks with a smile.

"Yes," Lucy replies kindly. Neither of them offers their hand because it's dark and the beginning of March, so they probably don't want to get frostbite. "Nice to meet you, Lukas."

His entire face lights up, the night sky brightening in his presence. He looks like a child that just got unlimited sweets, or an author that finally figured out *that* scene, or how she expects Alanis Morrissette felt when she wrote "Ironic."

He looks like he's realized she talks about him when he's not there.

"Nice to meet you as well. How was dinner?"

Lucy replies again as Sophie chews on her lower lip, thinking about a way to apologize to both of them for her inability to carry on a normal conversation.

"So tasty! Have you been to Bobby's?"

"No, but my Grams is desperate to go there! I'll take her this weekend."

Sophie shivers as an especially violent gust of wind goes past. Her scarf decides it's had enough of carrying the heavy load of keeping her warm, and the end falls to the floor in dramatic fashion. It doesn't reach the ground, thankfully, because that's gross.

Lukas is right there, his hand wrapped in red knitted wool. He pulls it back over her shoulder, maintaining a conversation with Lucy about who knows what. Sophie's never been very good at getting her brain to work when he's so close. He threads the end of her scarf through the other, forming a basic but sturdy loop. Not that she needed it right now—she's never been hotter a day in her life.

His knuckles graze the side of her neck, and she shivers with the contact, looking up at him just as he looks at her.

"Cold?" he asks.

"Mm-hmm," she replies.

"Sorry," Lucy pipes in, probably feeling the awkwardness flowing from Sophie's veins through their linked arms. "We talked so much at dinner, I'm not sure Sophie has a voice anymore."

"It's alright." He laughs and drops his hands from her scarf. "Mondays, right?"

"Yeah," Sophie replies, her arm rising as though she might reach for his lowering hand, but she doesn't. "Mondays."

"Well, I guess I'll have to try to see you tomorrow instead." He smiles.

He nods goodbye at Lucy as he walks past, his hand brushing Sophie's as he goes. She reaches for his fingers and he gives them to her, squeezing lightly as he turns his head back to smile at her.

"You know I'm right here," Lucy says with a laugh as they walk away.

"Don't even—"

"He's cute, SJ." She squeezes their linked arms together.

"Yeah, really cute." Sophie sighs.

"Is that a bad thing?" Lucy asks. It's not a bad thing, not even slightly. But it is terrifying.

"No, I don't think so," Sophie whispers, shaking the thoughts of what life would be like without him out of her head. She doesn't even know him that well, and she's too scared to ask. Why does he always leave at three p.m.? Who is Millie? She could probably figure it out if she thought about it, but she's not sure she wants to think about what it would mean for them if she's right.

"What shouldn't I get excited about?" Sophie asks, pulling the conversation back on track. Tonight was never about boys.

"Well, you know Cheriton Street?"

"Yeah, the road behind the shop," Sophie replies. It's cute, with nice gardens and large bay windows.

"I'm buying a house there."

"You're what?!"

Chapter Fourteen

It's a Saturday. The Saturday before Mother's Day, so Sophie should have been more prepared. She should have put the vacancy position in the window, and she should have done next month's order days ago, and she should have pre-wrapped some books before people turned up. The issue is, sometimes they want to check the books over before they buy them. That's their right, of course. Although sometimes Sophie thinks they might try to read the book before they gift it.

It's a genius move.

Lukas turned up about eight minutes ago, and Sophie hasn't been able to say anything to him at all. She sneaks a smile at him between customers when she can. He doesn't seem bothered. He potters around looking like he's made to be there, reshelving some books that people decided against and helping customers that don't really know what they're after.

In between customers, he says a quick hi and places his bag with her behind the counter. His hand rests on her lower back when he puts his bag down.

She messes up on the ribbon she's trying to tie.

Sophie knew she should have just thrown her hair up this morning, because now she's trying to gift wrap these books and blowing out the side of her mouth is doing nothing for the stubborn curls tickling her cheek. But no, she saw a hairstyle on Pinterest that she thought looked pretty (it does) but it's either wildly unpractical or she did it wrong (the latter more likely).

After the third shake of her head, she feels Lukas run his fingers lightly against her cheek and she thinks her chest might explode, but he does what she needed, tucking her hair behind her ear. He does it while maintaining conversation with another customer. He does it while seemingly unaware her heart is trying to crawl out of her ribcage.

He's gone before she can thank him, and she doesn't dare to look up from the task at hand because she's sure her customer is going to be staring at her with a smile she won't recover from, like everyone in the shop knows how unbelievably gone for him she is. The hair moves again, fortuitous in it's ability to annoy her.

Lukas is back before she knows it, his chilly finger behind her ears as he pulls her hair back. She wonders if he can feel her entire body heating up through her shirt. She wonders if her customer can see her bursting into flames.

Lukas continues to explain the difference between two children's books to a child no older than seven as he twists her hair behind her neck. It feels secure, like he does. It feels as though he's twisting himself into her life like there's never going to be a time when she doesn't look at something and see him.

"Thanks," she mutters, pulling at her bottom lip with her teeth when he's done.

"You're welcome, storm cloud."

Chapter Fifteen

"Hey, Soph," Lukas whisper-shouts from the door. Sophie looks up from her task. All four of the customers in the store look up as well. She wants to sink to the floor, but she wouldn't be able to see Lukas from there, so she stands her ground.

She doesn't like being called at, though, so she won't answer him. She does raise her eyebrow, and he laughs.

"Sorry," he says, coming into the store and closing the door. "I'm in a rush. I need to get to school. What are you doing tonight?"

"I have to do a stocktake," she grumbles. She wants to put it off because she wants to know what he's thinking about, but she's done that for the past three weeks and now she's not sure she's going to get it done in time at all.

"Eesh, every book in the store?" he asks.

"And the store cupboard." She groans as she throws her head back.

"Ouch. Sorry, Soph." Lukas checks his watch, and his eyes widen.

"School?" she asks, her eyebrows furrowed. Maybe he just means university. Sophie's pretty sure he's not a teacher. Maybe she knows why he goes to school.

"Mm-hmm," he says, grabbing his phone and typing something out. "Sorry, I'm late."

"It's okay," she replies with a shrug. She wants to ask him for his number, but in the time it takes her to gather up the courage, he's already out the door.

The evenings are finally getting light enough that if she had a long commute home, she'd enjoy the walk. The fact Sophie lives above her bookshop hinders that, but she thinks maybe on the weekend she could squeeze a walk in. Maybe she'll ask Lukas if he wants to go with her.

"Storm cloud," he calls out. She'd ignore him, but he is trying to speak to her over the obnoxiously loud music she has playing.

"Yes, sunshine," she replies. She hasn't seen him for at least twenty minutes because she got all the books out to count them and he turned up unannounced with pizza, so now they have to try to find each other in the maze of books and it's one of her favorite nights this year.

"Pizza break?"

"Mm-hmm."

She washes her hands in the small bathroom at the back of the store, and Lukas comes to do the same thing.

"There's not enough space, you savage!" She laughs when he shoves his hands between hers and the water.

"I don't know what you're on about. I'm getting clean right now," he replies, wiping the soap off her hands and onto his.

"You're so annoying." She smiles. He looks like he doesn't believe her.

He dries her hands for her, and she lets him, before he ushers her back out to the front of the store. There's nowhere to sit apart from her stool, so she lets him take it. She should have thought it through, though, because he picks her up and places her on his lap.

"You're not comfy," she lies as he wraps his hands around her waist.

"Get another stool then, Soph," he jokes. "I'm here for the long haul. Can your dad help you make another one?"

Sophie barely remembers that this seat has an engraving on the back of it for her from her dad. He helped her make it when she was a lanky preteen. It doesn't hurt to have it brought up like she thought it would, but she thinks it might leave a mark.

"It's just me and my mom," Sophie says, around a slice of pizza.

"Yeah?"

"Mm-hmm. My dad is somewhere with a different family," she states. She doesn't want sympathy, because she doesn't care that he's gone, but she prepares herself for it anyway.

"Sucks to be him," Lukas replies, though he does pull her a little closer.

"Loser." She laughs.

"He is," Lukas whispers, moving her hair over one shoulder. His lips soothe like a plaster.

It's silent again, and she wonders if she can ask him about his family, but she doesn't have to.

"Millie is my sister," he says, halfway through his second slice of pizza.

"Oh."

"But," he starts, swallowing against her back, "I'm her guardian. I have been for almost six years."

"What happened?" she asks, her thumb rubbing over the back of his hand.

"Car crash."

"Oh, I'm sorry, Luke," she says, getting up and turning to face him.

"It's been a long time," he replies, his hands resting against her waist. He opens his legs slightly as she steps closer.

"Still," she whispers, running her fingers through his hair. "Millie is lucky to have you."

"Mm-hmm." He laughs, though the action doesn't reach his eyes. "I wish they could have met you."

"Because I have fabulous taste in music?" she jokes, feeling a little unprepared for his words, though she's thankful for them all the same.

Besides, it makes him smile.

"That and your sterling dance moves."

"Oh, shut up," she says, pulling him into a hug. She's not sure why this is the first time she's had her arms around him, but she's also not sure she's ever going to let him go.

It's a little before midnight when the books are counted and there's only a handful of boxes left to put away. Sophie stretches, attempting to bend in a way that makes her back feel fifteen again. She catches Lukas watching her, a piece of paper in his hand.

"What's this?" she asks with a squint. She takes the paper from his hands, ignoring the shiver that runs through her spine as his fingertips linger on the back of her hand.

"Er, my resume, obviously."

She looks at the sheet, which has all of three words on it. It says "Hire me, please."

"You're ridiculous," she says, wondering if it would be weird if she stuck this to the fridge.

"Soph," he says with a laugh, then, "I'm here all the time. I love being here all the time, and honestly, I could probably just start working here anyway and it's not like you'd stop me."

"I wouldn't?" she challenges.

"Nope," he says. "You think I'm adorable."

"Ugh." She laughs. "Let it go!"

"I shan't! I'll take this one," he says, grabbing a box from the delivery pile. He rips the Scotch tape off the box and places it in the rubbish pile, then he dismantles the boxes and places them in a recycling pile, and she thinks she wouldn't mind if he stayed here forever.

"Luke—"

"It's not forever," he says, unloading the books. *Hell.* "Well, unless you want, just say the word, but you need to hire someone, and you don't want to do it without a trial, so you can just put aside the money you would pay—because I'm not taking a penny out your pretty hands—and you can figure out if the shop can afford someone for one day a week or three."

She pouts at him as he continues taking books out of the box, putting them into piles. It's what she would do, deciding which books go in which category before she actually shelves them. She wonders what his plan of action is. She wonders how he knows what she's thinking so clearly when she refuses to tell him the simplest of things.

"What's up, storm cloud?"

"Get out of my head," she grumbles, going to sit next to him so she can help him unload the box instead of doing any of the other jobs on her list. He kisses her on the temple.

"But I like it here."

Chapter Sixteen

It's a Wednesday when, for the first time, Sophie thinks she's falling in love with him. It's not something she lets herself think about if she can help it, but sometimes she doesn't have a choice.

Lukas paces around the shop, talking a mile a minute as he explains that he bought her something but it's not really something he bought more something he made but not with his own hands. She wants to tell him it's okay, she really just likes when he talks about it—but he hasn't taken a breath in about seven minutes.

His face is bright, even though it's miserable outside, and he bought her a hot chocolate already, and she wonders if that's the gift and if he knows he's already given it to her. But then he stops and pulls a small plastic container from his backpack. Sophie is still unaware of what it might be because she's flicking between watching his expression and looking at his hands.

"So, er, here," he says, holding the black plant pot toward her. She can see flecks of green coming out the top, and she thinks if he bought her a house plant, she might die on the spot.

"What is it?" she asks, walking around the counter to get closer to him. When she's close enough to get a clear look in the pot, she gets distracted by his face.

"I hope you like it," he whispers, though he doesn't answer her. He doesn't need to. When she looks, she knows exactly what it is. She's got them lined up on her windowsill in her apartment.

"A forget-me-not?" she asks, taking the pot from his hands and looking at the baggy green leaves. They won't have flowers yet, not for a few months, but she likes to watch them grow anyway.

"They're your favorites, and they're so tiny you can't get them in bouquets so I—well, I grew some."

"Yeah?" she asks, screwing up her nose because she thinks it'll stop her from tearing up. He places his hands on hers so they're holding the plant between them like some prodigal child.

"Well, I grew a lot. Did you know you're only supposed to put a few seeds in each pot?"

"Lukas!" she says with a laugh, and maybe a sniff.

"Don't worry. My Grams wanted some, and Millie wants to plant some in the garden, and—well, I killed a lot of them. Underwatering, according to Google."

"Ah, the dreaded underwater."

"Right?! A curse, truly."

She smiles at him, unable to do anything else. She wants to thank him, to tell him the plant is thoughtful and beautiful and everything she likes about him, but she can't.

Lukas doesn't seem to mind. He walks around the store, asking her questions about books he thinks she might like. (He also says all books should have a pretty cover, and she agrees.) He brings a stack to the counter, and they play a quick-fire round of "yes or no." It's apparently a game Lukas just decided upon, where he shows Sophie a cover and she says yes or no as to whether she would read it based on the cover alone.

It's fun.

(She doesn't tell him she's read all of them.)

It's a standard Wednesday with Lukas, really. He rubs her hands in his when she complains about being cold because she didn't put the heating on in time, and he listens to her talk about her favorite films (romcoms, obviously, because she doesn't like to cry over anything sad but she does choke up when Kat reads her poem to Patrick).

Lukas helps the customers that come in before Sophie has a second to register they've entered the store. He bounds around the place like a puppy when they know what they're after, and when he fist-bumps them when he finds the book they wanted, Sophie imagines cooking him breakfast. And when he slyly asks her questions about books when he doesn't know what book to suggest to customers (she always has a generic five to recommend if their questions don't give her anything to go on, but she'll share that with Lukas another day), she imagines waking up next to him.

And when he kneels on the floor of the shop to help a child choose between two different books, she thinks she's falling in love.

Chapter Seventeen

"What's your favorite book?" Lukas asks, pushing himself up on her desk with the palms of his hands. Sophie squints at him because she's not sure what he's getting at, but she does like the sparkle in his eye, so she relents. Kind of.

"Why?"

"Because I want to know." He pouts, and she's annoyed because when she sketched his face the other day, she missed the light dimple on the left side of his face.

She giggles like a schoolgirl but she lets herself not be embarrassed about it because he walks closer to the register, and she can't really be losing when he's this close. She can smell cologne on him that he definitely wasn't wearing the last time she saw him, but she can't call him out on it because she spritzed some perfume this morning just in case.

"Sophie," he groans, leaning closer, his palms heavy on the counter, and fuck, he has such good hands. "Please, will you tell me?"

"I'll tell you if you tell me why you want to know," she replies, slipping the straw of the iced tea he bought her into her mouth to stop herself from leaning up to kiss him.

"You're so . . ." He rolls his eyes as he smiles.

"So what, Lukas?" she asks, her eyebrow high. Lukas looks at her like he can hear the way her heart beats faster when he looks directly at her, or like he can see the blush on her cheeks even when the lights should block it out. Like he knows how crazy she is about him when he hasn't even asked for her number. She supposes she could ask, but if he said no, she's not sure she'd bounce back from that.

He leans forward, his eyes dropping only once as her heart claws its way up her throat. She's about to lean in, to let her nose brush his, to let herself finally figure out what he tastes like. But then he dips just as her eyes flutter, and he hears him slurp her drink through the straw.

"Oh my God!" She laughs with her head thrown back because he's got her wrapped around his little finger, and she thinks he knows it.

"Thanks, Soph," he says, his face still too close to hers for her to be able to function properly.

"You're an asshole," she says, pulling her drink back, though the way he smiles at her suggests he doesn't believe a word she's saying.

"If I tell you why I want to know, you'll definitely tell me?" he asks, his face suddenly nervous. It makes her stomach flutter.

"I said I would."

"I want to know because then I'll be able to figure out how to impress you," he says, way too fast for a casual conversation. How can he not tell he already impresses her? She could tell him, but he's already talking animatedly, his hands flying around.

"I don't want to get you flowers if you don't want flowers, though I have some more in my bag in case you do, and I thought maybe your favorite book would tell me if I should stand outside your apartment with a boombox in the middle of the night or maybe you'd like a picnic in the park or maybe I should try to paint you something—but just so you know, I can't paint at all, but I will try for you, or—"

"Lukas," she interrupts, feeling her heart about to burst with how reckless she feels as he looks at her. As he explains how badly he wants her to like him when she's already drawn his face an embarrassing amount of times.

"Sorry, is that too—that's too much, right? You're just so . . ."

"So what?" she asks.

"So crazy out of my league, Sophie. And not even because you're the most beautiful person I've ever seen, like, in my life," he says, his face turning pinker by the second, "but because you have a master's degree just because you were smart enough to get one and then a bookshop came on the market and you always wanted to own one so you just did it. You don't follow the crowd and you don't care what people think, and you can fucking draw like it's no big deal and you're so incredibly impressive that I don't know how to act around you because you make me feel like I'm going crazy every time you look at me. It's been like a month, Sophie, and I can't stop thinking about you. I don't know how to stop thinking about you."

He looks at her then, his face flushed, and he's blinking way too fast, his body heaving with the intensity of his words, and she likes him so much she wants to pull her chest apart and let him take whatever he wants. She's read the books. She's put in the hours rereading scenes and analyzing characters' words and actions. So, she should know how to act now. She should know how to reply and she should know how to tell him how she feels about him. But now that it's happening, she's so willfully unprepared because she never expected to be the one to hear them. Now she feels like those emotions can only be accessed through the words on a page.

"Soph," he whispers, his eyes wide as he stands in silence waiting for her to say something, anything, and she wants him to know she thinks about him too. That ever since she helped him with his exam she's thought about nothing but him, how it almost sent her crazy thinking about if he was going to come back and now that he's here she doesn't know how she ever coped without him, but she can't tell him all that yet.

So she does what she can.

"I care what you think," she says, biting her lower lip as he smiles at her.

"Yeah?"

She nods at him because it's all she can do, but he smiles.

"Okay, cool, that's cool," he says with a shrug.

"Loser," she replies.

She gets up and walks to her favorite section of her store, running her finger over the spines even though she knows what she's looking for and where it is. She plucks it from its place on the shelf and takes it with her heart back to the counter and picks up a pen.

"Are you allowed to write in books?" Lukas asks, his hands against the counter again as he clearly stands on his tiptoes to see what she's writing, but she'd rather die than show him.

"Go away," she says with a laugh, pushing his face lightly with her hand. He presses his lips to her palm, and she almost messes up what she's writing. And, *oh*. This is what she reads her favorite books for. This feeling in her stomach. This is what it feels like.

He winds his fingers through hers as she turns to look out the shop, his thumb rubbing against her knuckles. She's about to pull him back to her, to walk around the counter and just kiss him, but the sound of the door stops her.

"Hi, hello, good afternoon—" Tyler skids to a stop when he sees Lukas standing there. His gaze drops to their hands, and he smiles so wide Sophie groans and slides her fingers out of Lukas's because she is a professional and she can't deal with a teenage boy mocking her right now. She's too vulnerable.

"Afternoon, Tyler," Sophie says with a smile and probably red cheeks. She raises her eyebrows when he hasn't moved. Her having a boy—well, not a boyfriend but someone she clearly likes—isn't *that* shocking that Tyler should be stuck to the floor. Rude.

"Oh," he replies, walking toward the counter. "So, I know when I last came in you said that fancy book was *super* hard to get your hands on, which sucks, but then I saw it online, but . . ." He rests his skateboard against the front of her counter and runs his hand through his curly brown hair. "But I can't buy it online, SJ. I'd never do that to you. So, do you have any other recommendations?"

Tyler is adorable. Her favorite customer, even if Lukas is standing right here, watching them intently.

"SJ?" Lukas whispers, leaning his head toward her. Sophie just flicks his knuckles.

"I do. Or I have this," Sophie says to Tyler as she leans down and grabs *the* book from behind the counter. She watches Lukas peer over the counter with Tyler as if they don't know she's clearly got what he asked for. It took her ages and costs more than she'd ever make Tyler pay, but she doesn't mind.

"SJ! You got it!" Tyler says, freaking out. "You're the best! Amy is going to flip! Well, not *flip*, she's very cool, but she might smile at me."

Tyler continues tapping his hands against the counter before he walks over to her small selection of wrapping paper, his finger tapping his chin. Tyler is one of the most animated people Sophie knows, and she can picture all the ways his face moves as he tries to choose between eight patterns of wrapping paper, even though she can't see his face.

"What paper should I wrap it in? SJ, what would you pick? They're all recyclable, right?"

"Of course. What's Amy like?"

"She's kind of dark, insanely smart, super funny, she's real pretty too—kind of like you!" he says, as if it's a fact.

"Flattery will not make me wrap this for you," she replies. (She'll definitely wrap it for him.)

"SJ," he pleads, drawing out her nickname. "Please? It's for prom! Well, I want to ask her to prom, and if I ask her with a big show she'll definitely hit me, but she's wanted this book for so long, so I think she'd say yes. I mean, I think she'd say yes without the book too, but—" Sophie smiles at him, but Lukas speaks up first.

"You should get the one with skateboards and draw little hearts on it," he says.

"Hearts?! Man, I'm going for subtle," Tyler says, but he picks up the paper Lukas suggested anyway.

"Tyler, nothing about you is subtle," Sophie says with a laugh.

"Skateboards are cool—they'll remind her of you—and the hearts are cute," she says, looking briefly at Lukas. He's already looking at her like he was waiting to see if he picked correctly. She rolls her eyes at him.

"She doesn't like cute things," Tyler grumbles.

"All girls like cute things. You want a bow on it?" she asks while she lines the book up with the paper.

"Please," he says sulkily, then turns to Lukas. "She'll like the hearts?" he says.

"She'll like the hearts," Lukas replies.

"Hm. Well, if you can land SJ, then I guess I trust you."

Lukas laughs again as Sophie's jaw drops.

"I don't know," Lukas replies. "It took like two hours for her to tell me her favorite book."

"I haven't told you yet," she replies, adding another pink ribbon to the book—just to mess with Tyler, at this point.

"Well, I can't help you there. SJ likes me because she has no choice, I'd keep coming back anyway," Tyler says with a shrug. Sophie doesn't like it when people talk about her like she's not here, but this conversation is entirely too cute, and if she looks up right now they'd see her face is bright red.

"But she does hate everyone and everything, so if she lets you stay here for two hours at a time, I think you're fine."

"Okay, time to go," Sophie says, shoving the book into Tyler's hands. "Go get your girl."

"Thanks, SJ," he says brightly, then grabs his skateboard. He pushes his headphones back up, but when he gets to the door, he shouts back, "even though if I said she was *my* girl you'd throw me out! Bye, SJ's possible boyfriend who she won't tell me about!"

"Go away!" Sophie laughs.

She feels Lukas looking at her, so she chews on her bottom lip and looks around the shop. There must be something she needs to do. But then she feels his hand near her face, his fingers brushing some hair from her cheek as he tilts her face to his. His fingers linger behind her ear, and she's not sure how everything he does makes her feel like she's the lead in a novel she'd swoon over when he's barely touched her at all.

"You hating everyone and everything is not something that shocks me," he whispers with a smile. His thumb rubs over her temple as she checks his face for any semblance of a lie. She's not used to people wanting to get past her closed-off exterior, though she's also not used to wanting to show anyone what's behind it, either.

"I don't hate you," she whispers.

"No?"

"Everyone else but you."

"I can work with that," he says, his voice low as he leans forward but then jolts back. The family that just walked into the shop has *perfect* timing, just perfect, and she can overhear their need for numerous birthday gifts.

"I'll see you later?" Lukas asks, his lips against her forehead before she can blink, and she thinks hating everyone is fine, as long as there's someone she can love.

"Okay," she says with a smile, standing to help the frantic family. Her hands linger on her favorite book—a piece of herself she's terrified to give away but she will. Because it's not like falling when someone is there to catch you. She hands him the book, her phone number hidden on the first page, and his answering smile makes up for the snakes writhing in her chest.

Chapter Eighteen

Lukas texts her twenty-seven minutes later, not that she was counting.

Lukas: **Guess what I put you as in my phone.**
Lukas: **Guess guess guess!**

Sophie: **Storm cloud?**

Lukas: **You're so smart SJ.**

Sophie: **You remain the worst person I know.**

Lukas: **It also has a heart next to it, so maybe you're not the smartest person I know.**

Her real heart beats a little too fast.

Chapter Nineteen

Sophie is covered in a light shower of dust. Some of it mere hours old—those are the popular sections—and some of it a year old, from the last time she deep-cleaned the bookstore.

Lukas hasn't texted her. She needs a distraction. (Yes, she's aware she could get a grip, but she has texted him two different random questions and he hasn't replied, and she likes him way too much for him to not be texting her.) Sure, it's barely been three days, but he really should stop looking at her like that if he isn't planning on following through with any of the plans she's made for them in her head. He really should stop looking at her lips if he isn't going to kiss her, and he really should stop making her feel like she's in the middle of a romance novel if he's not going to give her the ending she wants.

She wants him to text her so she can ask him if he wants to go out on the weekend, and she wants him to text her so she can fall asleep rereading their conversations, and she wants him to text her because she wants to talk to him and she wants to know if he texts like he speaks, full of animation and emojis.

She just wants him to text her, and he's not. It's making her feel like she's back in high school, where she wanted to make friends but never could.

Also, there was a note on her door today (the bookshop, not her apartment, thankfully) but the rain washed away any of the ink so now either someone wanted to know when they opened or she has a stalker threatening to kill her, and she's none the wiser to which it is. So, she's ignoring it all for now. She's desperately trying to reach the book that fell and got wedged behind the bottom shelf sometime in the last few years, but she can't get her shoulder to bend the right way.

The doorbell goes, which is annoying, because she really was sure she flipped the sign to closed, and it's after dark, so really, can't people just leave her alone to ponder the boy she's falling way too hard for?

"We're closed, sorry," she says with a huff, refusing to show her face because she's so close to getting this book—if she could only dislocate her shoulder.

"Oh."

It's a little unreasonable how quickly her heart starts beating too fast at the fact Lukas is here. She'd recognize his voice anywhere, now, even with her head buried under the lowest shelf and her nose filled with dust.

"Are you alright?" he asks, his tone littered with something she can't place. She backs up, wriggling back on her knees until she can twist her head free. She's definitely going to be sore tomorrow, and she's not sure the lost book is even worth it.

"Yeah," she says with a moan, stretching her arms out in front of her to stretch her back out. "I lost a book like three years ago, and ugh . . ."

She tilts her face where she has it placed on the ground, the carpet scratching at her cheek, until she can see Lukas. He's gripping his backpack so tight she thinks it might rip, and his cheeks are flushed her favorite color, and his eyes are focused on something that is not her face.

Weir—oh.

Oh.

All too slowly, she remembers her positioning—with her bum in the air and her back arched.

"Erm," she says as she tries to rise from the floor, but her entire body feels stiff. Lukas is there in an instant, his eyes guilty as he drops his bag and helps her up, his hands soft yet sure against her waist.

"Are you sure you're alright?" he asks, knelt in front of her, as he pushes a lock of hair out of her face. He has a bruise above his cheek she wants to ask him about, but she's being attacked by a million dust particles right now.

"Yeah, I just—achoo!" She sneezes, her entire face scrunching. She manages to tilt her face to the ground, and he laughs at her, tilting her back toward him, his fingers light under her chin.

"Hi," he whispers, a small smile on his face.

"What?" she asks, knowing she must look utterly ridiculous.

"Nothing, you're just . . . cute."

His cheeks are pink again, and she swallows as she imagines how far down his chest it goes. But she can't look at him for too long in case she kisses him, when she really wants to ask where he's been and why he's got a bruise. But as she looks at him, she's distracted by the awe on his face and the pink of his nose.

"Shut up," she says with a smile, pushing his chest. He slides his hands into hers, holding them tightly as he helps her from the floor.

"You know you should probably lock the door if you don't want people to come in," he says, his hands still holding on to hers.

"I happen to like strays," she replies, her body arching into his without her consent, so she sways back. She drops his hands and throws her thumb over her shoulder, gesturing that she's going to get her keys.

"Erm, do you—are you staying?" she asks, stuttering embarrassingly as she gets to the door.

"I would love to be locked away with you," he says, his voice muffled.

"Nerd," she breathes.

She wills her heart to calm down as she puts her keys on the desk, forgetting why she needed them in the first place. She likes Lukas. She thinks he likes her, so she's really not sure what game he's playing with not texting her. Surely he knows her well enough to know she wouldn't like that. There really isn't anyone she knows that gets her as Lukas does, and it's barely been any time at all.

She walks back around and he's on the floor, the old book in his hand.

"Oh. Thanks," she says, distracted by the red of his cheeks. He smiles up at her, and she has to look away as he hands her the book. There are some stubborn webs on it, and she really should hoover behind the shelves at some point.

"So, what else needs doing?" he asks, jumping to his feet. The movement sends his top up, another jumper that looks far too soft, but it doesn't matter today because she's burdened with the knowledge of what that part of his stomach looks like and she feels a little wild with it.

"Er—"

"Soph?" he asks, his brows furrowed as he moves closer to her, his hand against her arm.

So she spins away, reaching for the top shelf that she knows she can't reach.

"I need—" She grunts, trying to reach the top shelf without getting the ladder because she only needs to put like four books up and the ladder is so far away. She should look into getting one with a railing that slides all around the store.

"What's up?" he asks, at her side in an instant, and she wants to thank him for his clear offer to help, but he won't be able to reach either.

"I just need to put these books up and I'm too lazy to get the ladder," she says with a sigh.

"Oh, okay, here," he says, standing behind her, his hands on her waist, and then he lifts.

"Oh my God," she squeals, as he lifts her effortlessly onto his shoulders. She fists her hand through his hair as he laughs at her, his hands on her knees.

"Is this okay?" he asks.

"Shouldn't I be asking you that?" she replies, her heart thundering in her chest. But he soothes her nerves as his hands slide up her thighs, holding her steady. "Aren't you hurt?"

"It's a slightly bruised eye, Sophie," he says with a laugh. She feels safe with him here. Even when he bends to grab the books for her, she knows he won't let her fall, and it's not like she doesn't like the feeling of his hands on her.

"You wanna dust while you're up there?" he asks, his thumb stroking her thigh.

"Mm-hmm. Are you okay?" she asks first.

"Ugh, I had a nightmare of a weekend," he replies, handing her the duster. "I took Millie to the butterfly museum, which was great—she loved it—but the tire on my car gave out. Well, I hit a curb trying to avoid running over a squirrel, so . . ."

"Aw," Sophie replies with a light laugh, running her free hand through his hair.

"So we had to stay in a hotel overnight, which actually turned out to be fun because we binge-watched Friends. It's the only thing Millie can watch that reminds her of our parents in a good way."

"That sounds lovely, Luke," Sophie whispers, brushing down the end of the shelf. She forgets to warn him to move back before he's covered in a light covering of dust.

He sneezes, and she laughs because he's entirely adorable, and she forgets to care if he texts her when he's right here. When she can imagine him liking her in the way she likes him. When she can imagine waking up with him and making lunch together. When she can imagine walking him to her apartment upstairs.

"You done?" he asks, his voice normal, like having her on his shoulder isn't an issue at all.

"Yeah, sorry."

He lifts her by her waist again, his thumbs resting against her spine as she floats through the air. Her feet hit the ground lightly, and he spins her to face him, his hands still heavy on her waist. Her breathing hitches when she looks at him, so close her nose almost brushes his.

"Hi."

"Hi," she replies, feeling far too breathless. She lets her hands rest against his chest, the hard muscles reaffirming what she already dreamt about. He's ripped. Her eyes flick to his, the slight bruise around his eye that she could have sworn was darker.

"Why are you bruised?" she asks, and he blanches slightly.

"Okay, so I broke my phone, and I didn't want you to think I was ignoring you, not that I was even sure you'd texted me, it was only three days, and it's not like I couldn't cope without talking to you—"

"Wait, what?" she asks, blinking rapidly, because she's basically been imagining her life as a spinster for the past two days. She thought he didn't want to talk to her, but she was clearly just in her clueless phase. Maybe like, chapter four or six or something, if she had to check.

He laughs nervously. "I just miss you when you're not around, and I wanted to talk to you, but it's—"

"You miss me?" she asks, her hands a little heavier on his chest as she lets her gaze drop to his lips.

"All the time."

"I miss you as well," she mutters, her nose brushing his as her eyes flutter closed.

The door opens, the bells chiming again, and she remembers how she went to get her keys to lock it but never quite managed it because Lukas was doing *something*.

"Motherfu—" Lukas mutters, resting his chin on top of her head as she laughs.

She's about to risk it all and kiss him regardless of whoever just walked in, until they hear, "Lukey!"

Chapter Twenty

Sophie whips her head around, unable to see who has come through the door, but with the look on Lukas's face, she could take a guess. She does see a car hovering outside the store with its hazards on, two elderly-looking people waving from the front seats. Sophie almost waves back but then remembers she's got no idea who they are.

"Oh, hi, Mills," he replies, a little breathless, if she had to guess. He waves to who Sophie assumes are the grandparents in the car. He doesn't drop his hold on Sophie's waist, though, and it makes her feel reckless.

"Grams and Pops dropped you off?"

"Yeah," Millie replies. "Sorry, um, they had—"

"It's alright," he replies sincerely. He drops his lips to Sophie's forehead and whispers that he'll be right back.

She watches him run to the car to drop a kiss on his grandma's cheek. She wants to know what they're saying, but when she hears "oops," she's reminded she has someone in the store.

"Hey," Sophie says, walking around the book stand. Millie is already sitting cross-legged on the floor, looking at the books suitable for teens and above.

"Hi, Sophie," Millie replies with a wave. She looks up quickly, then returns to her task at hand.

"You can call me SJ."

"This is a good one," Sophie says, pointing to Little Women. It was her favorite when she was reading teenage books at eight, under her duvet with a torch in the middle of the night. She sits down next to Millie.

"I haven't read that yet," Millie replies. "I have to check them all with Lukey."

"Well, that makes sense. They're a little old for you, huh?"

"Yeah, but as long as there are no bad words, Lukey doesn't mind me reading them. One time, he said yes and there were three bad words in it!"

"Oops! I guess he trusts you not to repeat them."

"He does trust me! And he didn't tell me not to tell you he walked into a lamppost when he was trying to get his phone to work so he could text you. So, I guess I can?"

Sophie laughs. It's a loud, undignified thing, and it makes Lukas whip his head around from where he's talking to his grandparents.

"He did?"

"Yes. We had to stop here last night so Lukey could put a note on the door." Millie laughs and picking another book from the shelf.

Lukas walks back into the store just in time to hear the end of Millie's sentence.

"Alright!" he says with a laugh, lightly pulling at her ponytail. She laughs, and Sophie feels all the better for it.

"Walked into a lamppost, huh?" Sophie asks, standing up from the floor. Lukas helps her up, his hand lightly against hers.

"Mills," he groans.

"I'm not lying just because you want to 'impress a pretty girl,'" Millie replies, her finger quotations looking out of place yet perfectly at home on a nine-turning-thirty-year-old girl.

"Pretty girl?" Sophie asks, a wide smile on her face as his cheeks turn pink.

"The prettiest," he states.

"Loser."

"Only for you." He laughs. "My er—my grandparents have a party to get to, so I've got to get Millie home. She's a grouch if she goes to bed past eight, and she's not had dinner yet," he says.

"I'm not hungry! I have books!" Millie yells, a struggle to her voice that suggests she's picked up even more books on her travels.

"Not even for pizza?"

"Gosh darn it," Sophie hears her whisper. "Pizza is so good."

"Sorry," Lukas whispers, just for Sophie.

"What for?" she asks, cocking her head to the side.

"I—I don't know. I haven't seen you in a few days, and don't tell anyone, but I've been miserable about it."

"I knew that," Millie states, walking over to them with at least ten books in her hands.

"Oh shush," Lukas says, but he laughs. "You can only get three!"

"Three?" she grumbles. Sophie is about to tell him she can take what she likes, but she doesn't want to undermine his authority.

"SJ, do you like pizza?" Millie asks, diligently trying to choose three books out of her pile of about fifteen.

"SJ?" Lukas exclaims. "How come she's allowed to call you SJ?"

"She asked." Sophie shrugs. "Anyway, of course I like pizza—I'm not an animal."

"Come with us!" Millie says.

"Oh," Sophie says, her eyes wide as her gaze lands on Lukas. He's chill as a cucumber, which is entirely rude because she feels like her knees might give out at any point. She's never even really been on a date with Lukas outside the store, but she wants to say yes.

"If you come with us, you can also bring three books," Millie adds, wiggling her eyebrows from her position of kneeling on the floor.

"Oh, er—"

"You can," Lukas replies with a small smile. It's a little nervous, if she had to guess. "If you want to, of course. I want you to come with us."

She's nervous, terrified even, as she always is when something new happens with Lukas. But she wants him. She wants to try new things for him.

"Yeah," she says breathlessly. "Okay."

Chapter Twenty-One

They decide the best idea is for Sophie to drive them to Lukas's place. Then she has a way to get home, and they don't have to take the bus at all. It makes sense because she's never even seen Lukas's house, and the thought of seeing it all and staying for dinner and staying overnight almost makes her miss that the light turned green.

Her playlist starts automatically, and she only turns it down so she can hear Lukas singing along under his breath. Millie reads the entire twenty-minute drive, and Sophie wonders if they're the only two people in the world that can read on car journeys without getting carsick. She always thought it was her superpower, but she doesn't mind sharing.

Lukas directs her flawlessly, telling her which lane to be in before the roundabout is in view. They're driving to a nice part of town, and she wonders if they're going straight past or if he lives in a fancy house.

"It's just this left, number thirty-six."

So, a fancy house it is. She wonders for a second how he bought one while still at university, but it only takes her about three seconds to remember the horrors that may have brought him to this part of town, and she feels awful.

"You can park next to my car," he says, pointing to the white car on his pebbled driveway. His house is pretty—all light brown brick and large white windowsills. She can see the smattering of forget-me-nots on the windowsill and the care that goes into the garden. It makes her heart feel full, and she doesn't feel half as nervous about holding his hand as he pulls her up to and then through his front door.

Lukas gives her a tour—a quick thing she thinks he does because it's polite more than him wanting to. The rooms are dated, and if she had to guess, they haven't been changed since his parents died. It makes sense, of course. These things are hard. She wants to know if he ever thought about changing them. If he's keeping them like this because he likes it or because he misses them too much. She wants to know every thought he's ever had.

Lukas goes to run Millie a bath, and Sophie takes the time to wander downstairs. There are countless photos on the mantelpiece, the walls, and the side tables. He looks a lot like his parents.

The kitchen is the only place in the house, apart from the garden, that feels like Lukas. Sophie's not sure if that's because the color palette is slightly different, or if this area feels lived in, like they could make a mess in here and it would be okay.

She smiles thinking about Lukas and Millie baking cookies in here, or maybe he helps her with her homework on the island while he makes dinner. There's a part of her that wonders if she'll ever get to do that with them.

That thought is shoved out of her mind when her gaze falls on the fridge. Usually, she'd nose around the fridge magnets (she likes to buy the tackiest fridge magnets she can find whenever she goes somewhere new), but all she can focus on are the bookmarks which line the side of the fridge. They're all there. He's completed his collection.

She wants to make another one, if only to keep him around forever.

"Your place is lovely," she says, as she bites into a slice of cold pizza. (It arrived a while ago, but Millie was talking her through her book collection and then Lukas ran a bath for her—she's in it right now—so she waited for him to get back downstairs before she ate.)

"Thanks," he mutters. "I want to update it a bit, but it feels ... I don't know, it feels rude."

"To your parents?" she asks, taking another bite of pizza.

"Yeah, I mean, it's been years," he scoffs, running his hand through his hair. "Millie doesn't really remember them at all and I'm nervous that changing her room will make them disappear from her mind entirely, but I—"

Sophie wipes her fingers on a napkin and grabs his hand. He winds their fingers together, his thumb smoothing over her knuckles.

"I know she'd like something different, you know?" he says. "She loves books, and they're all in piles on the floor because I'm terrified to cover up the wallpaper, and she's pink-crazy and everything in there is so dark and I—she's lost so much," he whispers. "I want to give her whatever she wants but I don't know how."

"Hey," Sophie says gently, pulling on his arm so he spins to face her on the couch. Her thigh overlaps with his. "She's got you. She's got the best big brother in the world," she stresses, her free hand against his cheek. "It doesn't matter what her bedroom looks like, all she really cares about is that you're there. That's all she wants."

"Yeah?" he asks as she runs her thumb under his eye.

"You don't have to do it all at once, but you don't have to keep everything the same to remember them. I already know they were kind, funny, and they raised the best person I've ever met—and I knew all of that before I saw your hallway floor."

"You're the best thing that's happened to me in a really long time," he whispers, pulling her into a hug, his hands tight against her back as she rests her chin over his shoulder.

"Thank you."

"Anytime, sunshine," she says, if only to make him smile, and when it works, she feels like she could conquer the world.

Chapter Twenty-Two

She's in love with him. He's reading Millie a bedtime story, doing three different voices, and she's in love with him.

Chapter Twenty-Three

Sophie doesn't tell Lukas that she loves him, because that's terrifying and she can barely even let herself be in love in her own head. She's avoiding calls from her mom because she knows she'll have figured it out (her mom thinks she's been in love with him from the start and she wasn't—she just liked him a lot). But now that she is? She's not sure what to do about it.

So, she does nothing. She texts Lucy back sporadically and she tells Lukas that work is so busy she can't see him in the evenings. She knows his class schedule for the last term of university is hectic, so she won't see him during the day as much.

She hasn't seen him since last Saturday evening, has barely spoken more than three words over text, and has been refusing to take his calls.

It's been two weeks.

And she's miserable.

It doesn't stop him from dropping a tea in on Thursday morning, though. She thanks him and holds onto his hand longer than she should, seeing as it's definitely her fault he looks that tired. She asks him how he is and how university is going, and it sounds so foreign to her that she barely remembers what he says—only the look in his eye that says he's as confused as she is.

He kisses her on the forehead and she feels like she's standing at the dock, shipping him off to another country. It feels like she might never see him again.

She's been known for her self-inflicted dramatics.

The days pass by—she's not sure how, she's not even sure what she's done—but there are some ticks on her to-do list, so she figures that's alright.

She reads a text from her mom telling her that Lukas won't be able to figure it all out on his own. That she owes it to herself and to him to at least let him know she *wants* to be able to talk to him about how she's feeling. She ends the text telling Sophie she's the greatest thing to ever live and that she loves her, but Sophie's not sure she's right.

When the clock hits six, Sophie decides to go home. She doesn't fancy being in her head for the entire evening, so she takes some old books to her apartment to fix the spines before she discounts them. She takes the back exit, even though she hates it. It's dark and it's where people keep their bins, so she convinces herself something lives behind them. (She did get scared by a badger once, but they're terrifying, so she allows herself to be nervous.) She could go around the front, but the rain is pouring down and going the back way saves her like four different locks, so she prepares to risk her life on the slippery steps.

The door slams behind her, and as she looks up from where she was walking (there's a step on the ground that's loose and if you stand on it your shoes fill with muddy street water), her eyes land on a hooded figure. She always thought in a fight-or-flight situation she'd run, because she's not getting hurt just to save face. As it turns out, she can't move.

Her body shakes, the box in her hands rattling as she tries to see through the heavy rain in the dark.

"Sophie?"

Oh. Even through the thundering of rain and the noise from the cars on the road, she'd recognize his voice anywhere.

"Lukas?" she asks.

"Soph," he repeats, stepping closer. There are no streetlights at the back of the store, but she never feels anything other than safe in his presence, so she lets him move until his body almost touches hers.

"You're getting soaked," he states. She knows this, obviously—she can feel the cold rain forcing itself down the back of her jacket.

"Yeah," she uselessly replies. "I was—what are you doing here?"

"I came to see you and the store was locked so I just—"

"It's alright," she says with a shiver. "Do you want to come in?"

"Yeah. Yeah. The store? I don't want to make anything wet."

"Upstairs," Sophie replies, and then, "I have some sweats you can have."

Chapter Twenty-Four

Lukas takes the box of books from her even though he has a heavy looking backpack, but she lets him because she needs to open the window.

She shoves it open, the frame acting up just to annoy her, and she climbs through. Sophie takes the box of books from Lukas, her fingertips brushing the backs of his hands.

"Thanks," he says with a sigh, the water dripping from his hair.

"Mm-hmm."

"You should lock your windows," he says, as he climbs over into her apartment.

"I don't think anyone else comes down here," she mutters, but she will get a better lock than the frames just being old and frustrating to move.

He shivers a little, leaning against her kitchen counter, and this really isn't how she expected him to see her place for the first time. She can't believe she fell in love with him before he even saw the inside of her apartment.

What a loser.

She looks at him as he drops his backpack to the floor. She wonders if he's got bricks in it, it's so heavy. Maybe he's bringing back all the books from Millie so he doesn't have to see her again if she's so hellbent on ignoring him.

"I'll er—grab some towels."

She shakes her coat off and quickly rings her hair out over the bath. When she gets back, she sees his head hanging slightly. The back of his hair is curly and wet and her chest aches because of course she fell in love with him. She's not sure how she couldn't.

She places the towels and spare clothes on the counter, lifting his head slightly with her hand under his chin. He looks tired, and a little sad. She doesn't know which one to address first, or if she even should.

She hovers, her hands itching to touch him, but she's not sure how, and she's not sure if she's allowed. He places his wet hand against her jumper and then immediately apologizes, taking his coat off. She hangs it over by the front door; the doormat will have to take the brunt of the water. When she turns around, Lukas is taking his jumper off. It appears his coat was not at all waterproof, and his jumper is sodden.

It all happens in slow motion. The way his biceps flex, and the way his T-shirt gets stuck to his jumper as he pulls. The way his abs move as he tries to fix the situation. The way her jaw drops open.

She walks over, brushes her fingers lightly against the hem of his T-shirt, and she does something she doesn't really want to do—she helps him pull it back down.

"What should I do?" she says.

"Nothing," he whispers, his eyes pleading with her for something, but she's not sure what.

"Lukas—"

"I'll dry, I don't need anything," he says, standing a little straighter as his hand lands on her waist again. Her jumper is dry for now, but it'll soak with her hair if she doesn't do something about it soon.

"Then what—what do you want me to do?" she asks, her hands against his chest as he leans toward her.

"Nothing, I just—"

"Luke," she gasps, her nose brushing his.

"Tell me you think about me as much as I think about you," he says, moving away from her and grabbing his bag. "I feel like I can never tell if you're looking at my lips or if I'm making it up. If you want to hold my hand but you don't because you want me to hold yours first. I don't know if me basically having a child is too much for you, because I'm terrified to ask. I don't know if you're ready to talk about it, and it's alright if you're not, but I am—" He paces, his voice frantic as he continues.

"I told myself to wait. Because I know you. I *know* you. And I know you need time and I know that talking about things isn't always something you want to do. And I get it. So, I waited, but you've been ignoring me for *weeks*, and I don't think it's because you don't want to be around me anymore. I think it's because you figured out what I've known for months."

"Lukas," she whispers, though there's no heat behind it.

"I have been trying to figure out how to tell you, because I couldn't do nothing—you deserve more than nothing. So I read all the books you've offhandedly mentioned you liked, and I wrote down everything I liked about them, but it wasn't enough. I thought maybe I could draw something, but I can't draw to save my life and Millie was no use whatsoever. I tried planting forget-me-nots in a heart shape in my front garden, but they spread like wildfire and there's no semblance of a pattern at all. I thought about making a scavenger hunt, but I couldn't even get you to reply to my texts, so how was I supposed to get you to the park? I knew you would hate if I said anything in public, so I haven't been dropping by the store because I'm not sure I could keep it in for another second."

"Luke . . ."

He brings the books out of his bag. They're wrapped in white paper, and she can see the bullet-point lists on the back (one says it has a pretty cover), and he sets them down on her kitchen worktop. They're stacked eight high, and she has no idea what books they are because they're fully covered, but when he spins them to face her, she doesn't care.

Along the spines are words, one word per book, and it reads *You're my favorite thing, and I love you.*

"It's okay if I'm not what you want," he says, his chest heaving as she reads the spines of the books over and over again. "But if I am, please tell me you love me back because I am going insane with it, Sophie."

Sophie can barely move, but she has to because he is what she wants. He's what she's always wanted. So she walks closer, her heartbeat racing with every step she takes. She walks until her nose brushes his and he gasps.

"I love you," she whispers in the space between their mouths. "I love you."

His lips touch hers, and she feels fireworks in her chest. His lips touch hers, and she wraps her arms around his neck to steady herself. His lips touch hers . . . and she feels like she's home.

Chapter Twenty-Five

"I can't believe you stole all those books from my shop and I didn't even realize," she says with a groan as she leans against him on her couch, tucking her feet under his legs.

"I could have got away with murder if I did it when I was standing a little too close to you," he jokes.

"Oh, shut up!"

Lukas laughs, pulling her closer to him with his hand on the underside of her thigh.

"I would have been able to read a whole lot more if you weren't constantly on my mind," he says, lifting her face to his.

"Okay. You just need to stop thinking about me for a second, huh?" she jokes.

"I don't know how."

"You're so dramatic," she whispers, her hand against his neck. He's cold—she should fix that.

"I am a romantic," he replies, pressing a kiss to her thumb when she strokes over his lip.

"Since when do you read romance novels?" she asks, leaning into him as he smooths his hand over her back. His fingers slip under her jumper, the feeling of his cold hands on her skin being the second reason why the movement makes her shiver.

"Since you told me they were your favorite," he says, his lips against hers finally. She's not sure there's ever been a book that describes the way it feels to have Lukas's lips slot between hers, to feel his hands bunching against her jumper as he tries desperately to get her closer.

"I love you," she breathes, ducking back to swallow his moan.

"I love you right back," he says, his hands tight against her waist. She lets her hands wander, and she lets herself dream of a life with him. Something that feels sure now she knows how he feels—though he showed her every day anyway. Life may not be a romance novel, but sometimes, you get lucky.

"Millie isn't an issue," Sophie says as she plays with his fingers. "Not that she ever . . . I just mean . . ."

"I know," Lukas replies with a smile. "We had a talk before I came here. You're not an issue for her, either."

"No?" She smiles. She wants to be as close to him as possible, and she's allowed now. So she shuffles closer, her knees touching his thigh. He rests his hand on her leg, and she's about to combust.

"Nah. She's been asking about you every day. I just—I had to make sure before I came here, you know? I knew I wanted you in my life, I just had to make sure my life wouldn't get in the way," he says with a shrug.

"It doesn't."

"I've never trusted someone like I trust you," he whispers. It makes her feel incredibly privileged and a little nervous.

"Mm-hmm," she replies. She wants to tell him something big, something profound, something that makes him understand how much she loves him.

"You don't have to say something just because I did," he whispers. "I'll always come back."

"I'll leave the window open."

"It's always open."

"You're the worst person I know," she says, laughing. But she'll keep him around for as long as she can anyway.

"I love you," he says, leaning his head against the sofa. "I just . . . want to tell you everything."

"Yeah?" she asks, feeling unprepared for the way he's going to love her. For the ways she knows he'll show her every day.

"Yeah," he replies. "I want to know everything about you. The things you find boring, the things you would never say out loud, the color of your thoughts . . . You make me want to read all the books in the world so I can figure out a way to express how I love you, because I can never find the words."

"Dork," she whispers, her eyes against her lap as he laughs at her, his palm squeezing her thigh.

She wants to find the words, but she mumbles. "I don't have—I'm not the best—"

"You're the best person I know," he whispers.

"Loser," she says with a laugh. "I won't be as forthcoming with everything, but I'm trying . . . I want to tell you everything as well."

"Yeah?" he asks, leaning closer to her.

"Mhmm. Like how badly I regret the last two weeks," she whispers.

"I forgive you," he replies casually.

"Yeah?"

"Yeah," he whispers, pulling her closer with a hand lightly against her ankle. He strokes over her foot while he clearly thinks about something and then he pulls her legs over his so she's sitting sideways in his lap, his arm around her waist.

Her heart thumps at his casual yet calculated movements, and she finds she can do nothing but look at his lips. She leans forward, her nose brushing his cheekbone as she moves him into the position she wants. For a moment, they breathe each other in, her lips barely touching his.

"Do you want to help me paint my office tomorrow?" he asks. Sophie places her hand against his neck, resting her forehead against his as she tries to get her breathing to slow.

"Yes," she murmurs, pressing her lips lightly to his. He repeats the action, covering her with short, light kisses.

"What color?" he asks, his hand slipping past the hem of her top. Her breath is choppy as she leans into him. She kisses him again, slightly longer but not long enough.

"Erm . . ."

"What's that?" he asks, maneuvering her until she's straddling his lap. It's better like this, with her legs on either side of his, his hands across her back, her shoulder blades, and her waist.

"Shut up," she whispers, parting her lips when she kisses him this time. Her hands are tight in his hair, their lips moving perfectly, if not a little frantic.

"You have to pick a color, SJ," he mutters, pulling her lower lip between his teeth. She moans quietly as his hand slips to the back of her neck, but she gathers he hears it by the way he pulls her against him.

"Pink."

"Dammit," he laughs. "I knew I'd get outnumbered."

"Get used to it, loser," she jokes, then says, "Can you stay?"

She feels his smile more than she sees it with how close she is to him.

"Let me check."

Sophie hands Lukas a mug of hot chocolate he didn't have to pay for as he warms up in her clothes, his mixed with hers in the washing machine.

"Thanks," he says, smiling softly at her as he places his phone on the coffee table. The screen is lit up, and she wonders if he just got a text that says he needs to leave soon. (He doesn't—Grams and Pops said they're fine to have Millie overnight.) He must see her looking because he lights up, grabs his phone, and shows her some images she doesn't quite understand.

"These are just some mockups. You can change anything you want, from size to color," he says excitedly. "So if I make a railing that sits behind the shelves at the top, and a loop over here," he says, pointing at the screen like she has any idea what he's talking about, "then you'll be able to reach any of the shelves—you just have to push the ladder."

"You're making me a ladder for the store?" she asks, her eyes wide as she takes the diagram in.

"Well, you can say no," he says with a gulp. "I just thought you might like one so you don't have to move the one from the back all the time."

"I love it," she whispers, feeling way too exposed because she never even told him she'd thought about it. He just gets her in a way she always hoped someone would.

"Well, I love you, so . . ." He shrugs and puts his phone back on the table. He says how he feels with such ease, and she wishes she could do the same back, but she has to trust he knows her well enough to know she'll tell him all the times she can.

"How do you even know how to do that?" she asks, knowing he isn't a carpenter by trade.

"My dad taught me," he says with a smile. "Most of the issue is being able to reach high enough and get heavy things into place. After that, it's simple math."

"Ah, just the heavy lifting and getting things into awkward positions, nothing major."

"Mm-hmm. I could have just told you my ladder plan from the beginning instead of thinking up random reasons to come into the store," he says with a laugh. "You have to know by now I only did it so I could see you."

"You could have just come to say hi," she says, and her lips brush his as he smiles at her.

"But I always want to be your favorite customer," he whispers, his lips against hers.

"You're my favorite person."

"That works for me. As long as I stay that way."

"Well, I love you and I hate everyone else," she says, pulling his lips back to hers.

"Everyone but me?"

"Yeah, everyone but you."

Epilogue

The leaves on the trees are a deep green, the air smells a little like vanilla and sunshine, and Sophie's bookstore door is always open. It's never been her favorite time of year, because sometimes her T-shirt sticks to her back if she's got to move a lot of boxes, and sometimes her fan doesn't cut it and she feels like she's in a sauna. But she's not mad at it. Not this year.

She watches children come through the store in shorts and sandals buying a new book for the summer holidays with their parents. She watches people walk past with bright ice lollies and ice cream dripping down their fingers (she has baby wipes and a bin on hand in case they try to walk into the shop). She watches smiling people in sundresses walk past like they're dancing, and everything feels a little better.

"SJ, can I put this here?" Millie asks, moving a plant pot closer to the window.

"Sure," Sophie replies with a smile. Millie wants to work in the shop at the weekend, but Sophie said she's not allowed because she's nine and that's probably a hundred human rights violations. But Millie ends up in the shop anyway, because Sophie likes to see her and she's a sucker.

Sophie doesn't mind, because Millie usually tries to do two tasks maximum before she throws herself on the tiny armchair Sophie bought especially for her and reads one to five books.

"I read up about them. They need direct sunlight," Millie replies, kicking her sandals off and placing them just under the chair. She sits up, a pile of books on her lap, and gets to work.

"Alright," Sophie says with a laugh, finishing up unboxing her latest bookmark. If she had to pick, this one would be her new favorite. She pulls them out, biting her lip to contain her smile as she does. They're sage green with light pink cherry blossom on them. It's a strange choice for her—anyone would think so if they looked at the colors and designs of the other bookmarks—but Lukas has a green jumper that's Sophie's favorite, and the cherry blossom reminds her of the blush on his chest and she feels a little wild when she sees him in it.

"Hey," Lukas says, strolling into the shop with a smile. "How are my favorite girls?"

Sophie rolls her eyes at him, and Millie gives him a half wave, but he doesn't seem to mind.

"She's midway through a chapter, huh?" he asks as he comes closer to the counter. "How has she been?" he adds, a little quieter.

"She's my favorite of the Martin family." She shrugs.

"Wow . . . Grams will be so hurt."

"Oh, shh," she says with a laugh, pushing his shoulder. He catches her hand and brushes his lips to her knuckles, as he does sometimes. It makes her breathing come a little choppy still, and she hopes it never stops.

"Hi, storm cloud," he whispers.

"Hey, sunshine," she replies. She leans forward quickly, pressing her lips to his. It's quick because Millie is here, and she swore she'd be more professional in her store when Lukas was around. But he's wearing a white crew-neck top, so it's a little difficult.

"Guess what?" he asks, her favorite smile threatening to break his face in half. He still has her hand in his, and it makes her brain feel too full.

"What's that?"

He pulls out a piece of paper. It looks more official than his résumé, which she has pinned to her fridge, but she opens it all the same.

"You passed?!"

"I passed," he says, somehow smiling even brighter.

"Luke, that's amazing!" She runs around the counter so she can throw her arms around him.

"Thank you," he whispers, his arms tight around her waist. "For everything."

"You were the one that sat the exam. You're the one that passed."

"Mm-hmm, but you got me the book, and you helped me study, and you—well, you're you." He shrugs as she pulls back.

"Loser," she breathes. "I'll take like, ninety-five percent of the credit, max!"

"Whatever you want," he says with a laugh, twirling one of her curls around his fingers. He's too close and too attractive for her to be able to stick to her rules about professionalism if she stands this close to him. So she pecks him on the lips, just once, then twirls out of his arms and stands behind the counter again.

Lukas looks at her like he might chase her, his eyes bright as they dance across her face, but then his gaze drops to the box of bookmarks, and he gasps.

"You made a new one?" he asks, his excitement through the roof, as if he didn't pass his course today. As if this is the only thing that matters now.

"I did."

"It's beautiful," he says, his finger running over the smooth finish. "The color is just like my jumper! You know the—"

"Yep," she replies with a pop of her lips. He squints at her, but she doesn't relent. It's not a lie if he doesn't ask.

Sophie busies herself with loading them into her display cabinet, leaning across the counter to do so. When she pulls back, Lukas has a five-pound note in his hand.

"What are you doing, loser?"

He picks it up, and she forgets about the routine. He's so ingrained in her life now that she can barely imagine going back to when they spoke for thirty seconds a day and she thought about it for the rest of her waking hours. She forgets the sparkle in his eyes and snakes writhing in her chest, until he says . . .

"One, please."

The End

About the Author

You can find **J.S. Jasper** on the following:

Instagram @jsjsprwrts

Tiktok @jsjsprwrts

Twitter @jsjsprwrts

Printed in Great Britain
by Amazon